"If I'm going to do this, you have to play by my rules," Derek said.

"Rule number one is we use first names. Rule number two is no getting emotional. This is just business. Nothing personal. Rule number three," he said, sitting down beside Chessey, "I give you thirty days of my life. Not a second longer."

Chessey drew in a sharp breath. Derek knew what she was thinking and he felt like a heel. She was thinking about their last kiss and whether she meant anything to him. He should explain.

He should tell her that she wasn't the kind of woman who could have an affair and say goodbye without a whisper of regret. And she certainly wasn't the kind of woman he could take home to live on a farm. And he wasn't the kind of man who could kiss a woman and not want more. A lot more.

It was better, far better, not to start.

ROMANCE

Dear Reader,

March roars in like a lion at Silhouette Romance, starting with popular author Susan Meier and *Husband from 9 to 5*, her exciting contribution to LOVING THE BOSS, a six-book series in which office romance leads to happily-ever-after. In this sparkling story, a bump on the head has a boss-loving woman believing she's married to the man of her dreams....

In March 1998, beloved author Diana Palmer launched VIRGIN BRIDES. This month, *Callaghan's Bride* not only marks the anniversary of this special Romance promotion, but it continues her wildly successful LONG, TALL TEXANS series! As a rule, hard-edged, hard-bodied Callaghan Hart distrusted sweet, virginal, starry-eyed young ladies. But ranch cook Tess Brady had this cowboy hankerin' to break all his rules.

Judy Christenberry's LUCKY CHARM SISTERS miniseries resumes with a warm, emotional pretend engagement story that might just lead to *A Ring for Cinderella*. When a jaded attorney delivers a very pregnant stranger's baby, he starts a journey toward healing...and making this woman his *Texas Bride*, the heartwarming new novel by Kate Thomas. In *Soldier and the Society Girl* by Vivian Leiber, the month's HE'S MY HERO selection, sparks fly when a true-blue, true-grit American hero requires the protocol services of a refined blue blood. A lone-wolf lawman meets his match in an indomitable schoolteacher—and her moonshining granny—in Gayle Kaye's *Sheriff Takes a Bride*, part of FAMILY MATTERS.

Enjoy this month's fantastic offerings, and make sure to return each and every month to Silhouette Romance!

Mary-Theresa Hussey

Mary-Theresa Hussey
Senior Editor, Silhouette Romance

Please address questions and book requests to:
Silhouette Reader Service
U.S.: 3010 Walden Ave., P.O. Box 1325, Buffalo, NY 14269
Canadian: P.O. Box 609, Fort Erie, Ont. L2A 5X3

SOLDIER AND THE SOCIETY GIRL

Vivian Leiber

Silhouette

ROMANCE™

Published by Silhouette Books

America's Publisher of Contemporary Romance

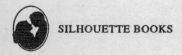

SILHOUETTE BOOKS

ISBN 0-373-19358-0

SOLDIER AND THE SOCIETY GIRL

Copyright © 1999 by ArLynn Leiber Presser

Printed in U.S.A.

Books by Vivian Leiber

Silhouette Romance

Casey's Flyboy #822
Goody Two-Shoes #871
Her Own Prince Charming #896
Safety of His Arms #1070
The Bewildered Wife #1237
The 6' 2", 200 lb. Challenge #1292
Soldier and the Society Girl #1358

VIVIAN LEIBER's

writing talent runs in the family. Her great-grandmother
wrote a popular collection of Civil War-era poetry, her
grandfather Fritz was an award-winning science fiction
writer and her father still writes science fiction and fantasy today. Vivian hopes that her two sons follow the
family tradition, but so far the older boy's ambition is to
be a construction worker and own a toy store, while the
other wants to be a truck driver.

Dear Reader,

Even with magazine and moisturizer labels exhorting me to defy my age or at least turn back the clock, I've always felt four hundred years too young. I'm meant for the days when a lady could turn to a knightly hero for protection, poetry…and passion.

But although I haven't seen any armored knights traipsing through my neighborhood or dragon slayers in my local supermarket, I'm starting to wonder if I'm just the right age for heroes. After all, there are heroes all around us. Like the paramedic who popped the quarter out of my son's throat, saving his life. Or the fireman who coaxed my elderly neighbor out of her house as its top floor burned. Or even the crossing guard who, day after day, makes sure that every child gets to school safely.

Silhouette is proudly honoring our modern-day American heroes, and I'm thrilled to be part of the celebration! My contribution to HE'S MY HERO! is Lieutenant Derek McKenna, a very traditional hero—he brought back his men alive from a dangerous mission overseas. But he's not very traditional when he's taking a gander at Chessey Banks Bailey's slim showgirl legs or when he's kissing her within an inch of her life in a Kentucky airfield, a State Department office or the White House!

Maybe I'm not so young. Maybe I could use a little of that moisturizer to defy my age. Maybe I was born at just the right time, the time of heroes in our own neighborhoods, heroes in our hometowns, Silhouette heroes. Open this book and meet Lieutenant Derek McKenna, a real hero. When you've finished the final chapter, walk down the street where you live—you might just meet another!

Best,

Vivian Leiber

Prologue

The head of the Joint Chiefs of Staff shrugged a thank-you to the secretary who placed his coffee on the low table in front of him even as he remained transfixed by the flickering images on the television screen set inside a bookshelf panel across the eighth-floor office of the State Department.

"I've watched this tape a hundred times over the weekend and I still get goose bumps," he said, leaning over a low-slung mahogany coffee table to get sugar for his coffee. "A hero. A real hero. Don't get too many of his type these days."

He dropped three cubes into his cup, affecting irritation when his aide reminded him that sugar had already been added. The general didn't like to admit that he really wanted six sugar cubes, more if possible. A sweet tooth was a weakness—he didn't have many.

"We've seen enough, I think," the congressman from New York said, flipping off the television set with the remote. An aide closed the armoire doors.

The congressman sat on a comfortable armchair by the window.

"I want this guy in Manhattan for the Fourth of July," he said.

"We get him in Washington," corrected the general. "Can't have a hero in New York on the Fourth of July—he's got to be in his nation's capital."

The New York congressman narrowed his eyes.

Winston Fairchild III pulled a sheaf of papers from a manila envelope and cleared his throat to get the meeting started. The group was ordinarily of a type not given to listening. In addition to the general and his aide, an assistant undersecretary to the Defense secretary had been sent over by the White House, and three congressmen who held key chairmanships of committees affecting the military had asked to attend. His office facing Twenty-third Street had been transformed into a gentleman's tea party, with real china instead of foam cups and dainty pastries instead of the stale bagels sold at the basement cafeteria.

But while it all looked very cozy, this was a

serious meeting about a serious opportunity and everyone was paying close attention to the soft-spoken Fairchild because he had something that everyone wanted—a real-life honest-to-God true blue American hero.

Winston was descended from a long line of behind-the-scenes advisers—his great-great-great-grandfather had served as George Washington's aide-de-camp, his great-grandfather had advised Lincoln to shave his mustache, and his father had told Franklin Delano Roosevelt that cigars were bad for his health. Fairchilds had seen generals and presidents come and go. Winston had some perspective on the men gathered in his office—any one of them could be retired, disgraced, dishonored or just plain tired of Washington within the year.

But a hero! A little of the stardust of heroism could rub off on any or all of these men and a career could be made.

"McKenna could reinvigorate the military's image," murmured the honorable congressman from Arizona. "We sure need that."

"Absolutely," the general snorted.

"Let's begin, shall we? Lieutenant Derek McKenna is thirty-three years old," Winston said, nodding to the summer intern to pass out copies of the fact sheet he had prepared over the weekend. He pulled his wire-rimmed glasses from a small tortoise case. "He was born and raised in Ken-

tucky on a farm in the mountains between Elizabethtown and Bowling Green.''

"E'town," corrected the general.

"Pardon?"

"Kentucky folks call it E'town," the general
said. "You don't pronounce the *L*, the *I*, the *Z*, the
A, the *B*, the *E*, the *T* or the *H*."

"I see," Winston said, and dutifully crossed out
the unnecessary letters on his copy of his report.
"Thank you, General. Now, continuing, he received good grades in school, but dropped out of
his first year in college at Bowling Green Univer-
sity in order to help his father on the farm. Two
years later, the farm back in order, he joined the
Army. He is a career soldier with a distinguished
record. A list of his medals is Appendix B on page
seven of your handout."

Everyone except the general turned to page
seven.

"And then there was Iraq," Winston said.

An uncomfortable silence. Everyone knew about
Iraq and the terrible fate that had befallen Mc-
Kenna and his men. Part of the team sent in to
help with humanitarian relief for Kurdish rebels on
the border with Turkey, he and his men had been
presumed killed in a firefight with Iraqi Republican
guards. A United Nations resolution condemning
the killings, the President expressing outrage in his
weekly radio address, a Congressional team of ne-

gotiators failing to get the bodies back, a darkly foreboding article in the *New York Times* and then...nothing.

Lieutenant McKenna's story faded from public consciousness, replaced with the Los Angeles celebrity trial of the week and new scandals at the upper reaches of government.

Until last week, when Derek McKenna—sporting a chest-grazing beard, a tobacco-colored tan, native *chuprah* dress and a haircut as crude as a caveman's—stepped across the Turkish border. He led his men, having not lost a single one, on an impossible journey to freedom from a Baghdad prison. By the time the Wiesbaden military hospital in Germany gave him a haircut, lent him a razor and issued him a new uniform, America remembered it had a hero. The television news conference from Wiesbaden where Derek McKenna announced that all he wanted was to go home and live a quiet life had put a lump in the throat of the most cynical of Americans.

And the men gathered in the well-appointed State Department offices knew they had a solid gold, all-American, apple-pie opportunity.

"The President's position is that we have him by rights," the undersecretary said. "We put him on every news outlet, every parade, every ribbon-cutting ceremony, every graduating class..."

"And every campaign fund-raiser?" the general asked archly. "After all, this is an election year."

"No, of course not," the undersecretary said, placing his hand over his heart as if to quell his outrage. "But we can at least agree that we all want a piece of him. The only question is how to divide the hero pie, right, gentlemen?"

The men gathered around the low table nodded, and Winston, sensing that his briefing on McKenna's attributes was over, laid a large appointment calendar on a space he cleared of clutter.

"Gentlemen," he said, shoving his glasses to the bridge of his nose. "May I present Derek McKenna?"

And for the next four hours, the men argued, cajoled, coerced, ranted, threatened and bargained behind the locked doors of the office of Winston Fairchild III until they had every minute of Lieutenant Derek McKenna's next six months accounted for.

Chapter One

"No," said Lieutenant Derek McKenna.

He looked around the swank State Department corner office. The men he addressed hadn't quite absorbed the word he had uttered, but their baffled expressions suggested their brains were working feverishly. Derek would be patient—after all, no wasn't a word any of these men heard all that often.

Any right-thinking soldier would be scared to tell the gathering that he wasn't going along with their carefully laid plans. Who was Derek McKenna to say no to the general at the helm of the Joint Chiefs of Staff, two congressmen, several State Department officials and somebody from the White House who had been identified as the undersecretary of the undersecretary of the chairman of something that had been lost in the rush of handshakes and salutes that had started this meeting?

But Derek had spent two years in hell and wasn't scared of a few suits or a chestful of medals.

"No," Derek repeated, in case anyone in this room still didn't get it.

They didn't.

Just stared at him, the congressmen from New York worrying a pencil with his teeth, a bubble of dribble erupting on the open mouth of the congressman from Arizona, the State Department official whose office this was rubbing his glasses on his tie.

"Did you say no, son?" the head of the Joint Chiefs of Staff asked.

"Yes, sir. I mean, that was a no, sir," Derek said. And then he lifted his chin, challenging the general to disagree. He was going back to the farm. No more of this see-the-world, broaden-your-horizons, more-to-life-than-this for him.

Kentucky was just fine.

"I said no and, with all due respect, General, I meant it," Derek said. He shoved the appointment calendar off his lap. An aide rushed to pick it up. "I'm not doing any of this."

"But, soldier..."

"General, I didn't dream every night in my

prison cell about going on Barbara Walters or hitting the rubber chicken lecture circuit or even having dinner at the White House and getting a photo op with the first family. I didn't dream of shaking hands, parades or even giving stump speeches to the League of Women Voters.''

Actually, Derek had spent most of his daydreams back in the green, lush fields of Kentucky. Planting and replanting in his head the plot of land that belonged to his father. Feeling the soft tender shoots in his hands. Smelling the heavy, damp air of morning. Hearing the cicadas' nighttime mating call and the creak of the rocking chair on the front porch.

Sometimes his dreams had been so real, so fresh, so vibrant that he had thought the hellish prison cell was itself the dream and that he could awaken. A deep and brooding loneliness would overtake him when he would realize the truth. That he couldn't awaken, he could only endure. And find a way out.

The fact that he was in Washington was proof enough to these men that he had indeed found a way out.

But Derek knew they were wrong.

And that's why he had to say no.

"Besides," Derek added, bringing out his trump card with a devilish smile. He had figured this one out about six months into his captivity. "General, you can't tell me what to do because my enlistment expired while I was away.''

A bespectacled suit who had been seated in a folding chair next to the ficus plant pulled a yellow legal pad out of a briefcase.

''Joe Morris, Justice Department,'' he introduced himself. ''Lieutenant McKenna, a soldier may be called back to active duty or held back from a discharge under special circumstances.''

Morris glanced at his notes.

''The case of Green versus Grant is most instructive on this point,'' he said. ''And I'll just read you a quote from the Supreme Court opinion. Justice Thomas, writing on behalf of the court, states that—''

''I don't think we need the legal mumbo jumbo at this point,'' the general interrupted. Joe Morris looked crestfallen, having lost his moment to show off what he had produced in a week of research into legal lore. ''Just give us the bottom line.''

''The bottom line, sir?''

''Yes, the special circumstances.''

Morris swallowed and then looked at Derek.

''All it takes is a request from the President to reinstate you, Lieutenant. And he can actually reactivate the request repeatedly, for as long as he feels that your services are required for the national interest. In other words, as the Supreme Court stated—''

"Get the President on the phone," the general told his aide, slyly adding another cube of sugar to his coffee.

Derek lifted his hand. The aide hesitated, a slim, manicured hand held aloft at the phone.

"All right, fine, I'll give you two weeks if you don't call," he said.

"Three months," the general countered.

"A month."

"All right, a month, but we're going to shuffle this schedule so that it's heavy. Very heavy. That means appearances every day."

Winston leaned his head back and signaled to his aide.

"Get an alternate schedule produced stat."

"Yes, sir. I'll have it by tomorrow, sir."

"No, you'll sit down at my desk right now and put it together while we wait. A month divided into three-hour appearances, four a day, comes out to…"

"Fairchild, even combat soldiers get some rotation time," Derek said.

"This isn't war," the general said archly. "This is a pleasure."

"A pleasure in which I'm not so sure I want to indulge," Derek said, leaning back in the comfortable pillows on the couch. He lifted his boots, noting with joyful mischief that they carried just a few drops of tar from the recently repaved streets of Washington. "I'm willing to start next week."

"Tomorrow, soldier."

"Three days from now."

"Hey!" Winston exclaimed. "You can't put your feet there. That table was purchased by the wife of Martin Van Buren! It's a national treasure."

The upper-floor offices of the drably modern State Department building had been recently refurbished with elegant furniture, rugs, paintings and fixtures from the early 1800s.

Derek crossed his boots comfortably on the priceless table. A globule of tar was dislodged from the sole of his right boot and dropped onto the leather writing pad of the congressman from Arizona before he could snatch it away. Ignoring the elected official's distress, Derek snagged a soda can from a hospitality tray next to the couch.

"Can I borrow your pen?" he asked the Justice Department lawyer. Joe Morris held out a Mont Blanc.

"My mother gave it to me as a graduation present," he explained.

Derek rejected it in favor of a disposable ballpoint in the hands of the undersecretary.

He turned the pop can over and stabbed the pen's point into its bottom. Then, holding the can aloft so that the tab was scant inches from his open mouth, he popped it open and removed the pen. The soda shot downward in a violent stream. Derek's Adam's apple bobbed only five times as he swallowed the entire contents of the can.

He had had two years to practice this chugging method, learned in college but then fallen into disuse. But the Iraqis love American colas and chess. Coached by his men, Derek had become a master of the latter in order to bargain for the former. He and his men had been living on sodas, smuggled-in food and a strong solidarity. The small pleasures and fun they created daily had been their salvation in a hell that civilization forgot.

Still, he could be a gentleman if he wanted.

But for his purposes, being a gentleman didn't suit.

After emptying the can, he put it on the hospitality tray. He returned the pen.

And then he let loose a burp.

Not a grotesque burp, but loud, clearly satisfying and utterly unrepentant.

"Mr. Fairchild, are you sure you want me to continue working on this calendar?" the aide said.

Her words hung in the air. Winston stared in horror. Derek shifted his crossed legs just a bit so that another drop of Washington street tar dive-bombed onto Mrs. Martin Van Buren's precious coffee table.

"Don't you think it would be a mistake to send

me anywhere?'' he asked, letting loose another burp. Resisting the urge to put his hand over his mouth.

''General, maybe this isn't such a good idea. After all, he's not housebroken,'' the representative from Arizona pointed out. ''He could do anything out there.''

''I could,'' Derek agreed and burped for emphasis.

''He does that once on *Larry King Live* and we've got a real situation,'' the undersecretary said.

The congressman from New York gnawed at his pencil.

The general glared at Derek, willing him into an embarrassed apology.

''Soldier,'' he warned.

''General,'' Winston Fairchild said, leaning forward in his seat. ''If I might offer a possible solution...''

''What?'' the general snarled.

''Call Protocol,'' Winston said to his aide. ''Get Chessey Banks Bailey on the phone. Gentleman, this man needs the functional equivalent of Mary Poppins.''

On the other side of the building, in a basement office of an annex to an annex with a single six-inch-square dusty window near its ceiling, Chessey

Banks Bailey arranged ten linen envelopes on her gunmetal government-issue desk. Each proper and perfect envelope had her name on it, and each one posed a problem.

Chessey was a Banks Bailey of the Banks Baileys whose ancestors crossed over on the *Mayflower*, the same Baileys that had made a fortune in diamonds or furs or maybe it was farming—but it was so far in the past that no one could remember. However, the family members were pleased with the way their money doubled and tripled and quadrupled over the years. Banks Bailey women appeared regularly in the pages of *Town & Country*. Their husbands were featured in *Forbes* and *Fortune*. Their homes in *House Beautiful* and their pets in *Pedigree*.

It would have been a surprise to the columnists of any of these papers to learn that none of the Banks Bailey money had ended up in Chessey's purse.

The linen envelopes were this June's invitations to family weddings and christenings and dinner parties. For each and every one of them, Chessey would come up with something to wear and something to give. The former was not too much of a problem, because her cousins were quite generous about last year's clothes. Although the Chanel suits and dresses by Dior ran short because Chessey inherited her legs from her mother, Chessey kept these hand-me-downs neatly mended and pressed. She was quite confident that she'd manage to have something appropriate to wear for every occasion she was duty-bound to attend.

The second problem, what to give, was more daunting. Her cousins had, in quite rapid succession upon reaching their twenties, married men of highly developed pedigrees and portfolios. Chessey was always thrilled by love matches and considered the fact that every cousin had married a millionaire a wondrous statistical oddity. Still, weddings required a gift and millionaires marrying Baileys expected more than a toaster from the local housewares store. And christenings—well, something engraved was always nice. She snuck a peek at her checking account balance.

In a toss-up between eating and presents, she'd pick presents. Besides, she could always make up for her choices by eating well at the parties. She made a list of the RSVP's she'd have to return, the presents to select and the times of all these events.

She picked up her phone on its first ring. "Good morning, Chessey Banks Bailey, Protocol."

"Get up to the eighth floor, stat," a voice snarled and then hung up without waiting for a reply.

She recognized the trademark charm of her boss's aide.

"Good morning to you, too," she said to the dial tone. "I'm just fine, and how are you?"

She put down the phone.

A summons to Winston Fairchild's office. She made a quick check of her lipstick, satisfied that none of it had ended up on her teeth. Then she grabbed her briefcase, on impulse throwing in her clutch purse.

Winston Fairchild III. Everything a woman could want in a man. Intelligent, refined, cultured. A Harvard graduate. Distinguished family. He was exactly the kind of man her family would welcome for Sunday dinners, holiday weekends. So suitable that she might even be considered a normal Banks Bailey were he escorting her. Even her grandmother had asked her why she didn't invite him to the family compound.

Chessey allowed herself the briefest of fantasies. A fantasy involving classical music, reading the hefty Sunday *New York Times* together, drinking cappuccino.

Completely unattainable, Chessey concluded, knowing that she was not like any other Banks Bailey cousin and therefore Winston Fairchild had a habit of looking at a point just above her head, far, far away, whenever they passed each other in the hallway.

Chessey knocked first on the wood paneled door and, on hearing a vague response, entered the corner office. She had only been summoned once before, two years ago for Winston Fairchild III's one-minute "glad to have you on board at the State Department, fill out your withholding form at my secretary's desk" talk. She noted that the ficus in the enamel planter still looked dead.

The office was more crowded than she remembered.

The head of the Joint Chiefs of Staff, two congressmen and a Defense Department undersecretary. Chessey quickly recovered from her gee-whiz reflex. She held out a slim, manicured hand to introduce herself to the general, Winston having conceded the duty with a vague you-know-everyone-here wave.

As she exchanged introductions with the New York representative, she saw what looked to be a circus performer with his feet up on the table.

He slouched against the cushions of the chintz couch and reared his head back to catch the peanuts he threw in the air. He never missed. After four such dazzling feats, while explaining to the horrified congressman from Arizona that he once did this two hundred times in a row, the performer did a double take in her direction. A peanut landed in his lap.

He was breathtakingly handsome—but only if you went in for strong, primitive types. The kind with hard, square jaws. Frankly appraising blue eyes. Sharply defined muscles. Coarse, callused hands. Incongruously boyish smiles.

Which Chessey didn't.

She stood a little closer to Winston, whose scent was familiar because she had smelled it just the day before on a scent strip in *Town & Country* magazine.

"I haven't had the pleasure of meeting you," she said, holding out her right hand to the stranger. "Chessey Banks Bailey."

Rather than shake, he gave her the once-over—twice—and then howled.

"Whooee! I knew there was something I've been missing for the past two years!"

His words were delivered with an inappropriate leer. Chessey bristled and then gaped first in reproach and then astonishment.

"You're Lieutenant Derek McKenna!" she exclaimed.

"One and the same, darlin'," he said. He uncrossed his ankles, dropped his boots to the floor and rose to take her into his arms.

Before she could marshal a protest, he kissed her. Full on the lips, enduring her small fists against his chest as he would an annoying but helpless fly. His mouth possessed hers, claimed her as the spoils of a conquering hero and when he abruptly let her go, she felt strangely bereft, as if she were a doll cherished and then discarded by a child.

She steadied herself with a hand on the back of the wing chair in which Winston sat.

If she had been given time enough to hope that Winston would come to her aid with gentlemanly rebuke, she was to be disappointed.

He said nothing.

Kisses like this didn't happen to Baileys.

Nor, she would suspect, to Fairchilds.

She wondered if Winston might harbor the ridiculous notion that she had provoked the lieutenant. If she were at fault for this appalling behavior. The other men were shocked—shocked!—but they gave her no mind. Indeed, their eyes followed Derek, who sprawled on the couch.

Winston, on the other hand, shook his head disapprovingly.

"Totally untrainable," Lieutenant McKenna announced. "Not suitable for American audiences. Bound to cause more trouble than I'm worth."

"Soldier," the general said sternly.

Chessey touched her chest to still her galloping heart. Shock was being replaced with outrage, outrage that was all the more potent because it contained the niggling iota of attraction. McKenna barely noticed her, which made her outrage spiral upward like a tornado.

He had no right, no right at all!

"You don't want me, General," Derek pleaded. "First time I land a kiss like that on a Junior League matron, you'll have to hide your head in shame for having set me loose."

"Soldier," the general repeated. "I've had enough of this nonsense."

"I'm telling you, send me home," McKenna said, with enough pleading in his voice that some of the men looked at their shoes, a single spark of decency within them realizing the unfairness of asking a man who had given so much for his country to simply do more.

And Chessey's outrage deflated into a puddle of bewildered pity. He was clearly suffering. A man in pain. All that he went through... Whether from some kind of posttraumatic disorder or the simple and honest longing homesickness, he simply wasn't in possession of his senses.

But he kissed me! Her outrage whimpered. *He humiliated me in front of these men! And in front of Winston!*

The general nodded in her direction.

"Ms. Banks Bailey, you deserve an apology for that behavior," he said. "But I suspect this soldier isn't going to give it to you. So I will. I am very sorry. He's acting like a savage."

"That's why we need Chessey," Winston said.

Need me? Chessey sat on the oak captain's chair beside Winston. He handed her a briefing folder.

The aide behind the desk passed her a calendar covered with pencil scribbles.

"Soldier, you're going out there for one reason and only one reason," the general said.

"And just what is that reason?"

"Because the enlisted men need you," the general said evenly. "The enlisted men need to know that officers like you will lead them out of harm's way and that officers like you won't leave a man behind."

"They already know that, just because we're out of there," he said. "I'm leaving."

He stood up.

"Get the President on the phone."

Derek uttered an oath.

"Give him the schedule."

Winston handed McKenna the appointment calendar, which matched Chessey's.

"We can play around with the dates so that you begin in three days," Winston said. "And Chessey will be with you. You've already introduced yourself. Next time you want to introduce yourself to a woman, try shaking hands."

Chessey endured McKenna's frankly hostile gaze. It was hard to believe that moments before, they had been locked in an intimate embrace.

"Why do I have to take her with me?"

"She's an assistant protocol specialist," Winston said. "You need to be housebroken. She's the best, like Mary Poppins without an umbrella and that silly hat. Trained the entire delegation to Zanzibar last month on how Zanzibarian table customs work.''

Chessey squelched a smile at the praise.

But Mary Poppins?

''And she's a member of the Banks Bailey family,'' Winston continued. ''Can't get a better pedigree than that. If there's a right way to do it, the Banks Bailey family knows how—whether it's tea parties, formal dinners, receptions or meeting a Queen.''

''I don't need her,'' McKenna said, gazing at Chessey levelly. ''On my farm, she won't do me any good milkin' cows or driving a tractor. And even if I were to go off on your little tour of America, I'd prefer a woman who looks a little less wholesome than this Girl Scout.''

The gathering stared at Chessey, seeming to expect her to suddenly make a fire out of two sticks or sprout a green sash. Chessey felt a crimson blush flare on her cheeks.

''If Lieutenant McKenna needs a party girl to accompany him,'' she said, ''I am certainly not the appropriate choice.''

''Party girls he can get anywhere,'' the general snorted. ''He needs to be returned to a civilized state—being in that Baghdad prison must have warped him.''

"Or maybe he was always this primitive," Winston observed. "In which case, Chessey, you've got a lot of work to do."

"I won't disappoint you."

"I don't want this woman," McKenna said, looking at her. "Even if I was going on your tour, I wouldn't take her."

"Soldier, we know you're not going to embarrass us with a cross-country display of your soda chugging and peanut tossing abilities," the general said. "And I can only hope that you're not going to kiss every single female in your path. But the schedule does present some very different experiences for you. Different social stratas."

"Excuse me, General," Chessey said, looking up from the folder. "My assignment is to go on the road, alone, with him?"

"Think of yourself as an animal trainer," Winston said.

The general chuckled. "My guess is that if you succeed at housebreaking this hero, you can pretty much pick your job here at the State Department," he said. "Am I right?"

"Absolutely," Winston agreed. "All he needs is a dress uniform, a stump speech you can toss off in a minute, and a quick, but thorough, course in manners."

She stared at McKenna bluntly.

Definitely the manners. He needed the manners.

"I can have any job?" she asked.

Winston started to mumble about civil service requirements.

"I think the fine state of Arizona would be delighted to have you on board in its congressional offices," the congressman from Arizona said. "How about New York?"

The New York congressman bobbed his head.

"If you pull this one off, you can have my job," added the general.

"Chessey," Winston said, in a voice soft as suede. "I'm counting on you."

"You are?"

"Absolutely," he said, and he took off his glasses. When his big brown eyes gazed into hers, Chessey felt as if he were seeing her—really seeing her—for the very first time. "Chessey, your country...I mean, I really need you."

She looked down modestly but then did a one-eighty, boldly meeting his gaze.

Such a nice man, her grandmother had said once, when Chessey had described her job.

"The Fairchilds don't have money," her grandmother had added wistfully. "But they have more than made up for it in good breeding."

"That settles it," Chessey said. She looked at her charge boldly, determined to make sure the balance of power was established early. He hadn't had the luxury of the good breeding of the Fairchild family, but he could learn. And she could teach him. "Lieutenant, we will start with lesson one. You are never to kiss me again."

And she swept out of the room.

Not quickly enough to avoid hearing his reply.

"All right, all right, I'll wait till you ask me."

Chapter Two

"We'll start with the uniform," Chessey said, leafing through the schedule folder as she led him down the linoleum-tiled hall. Her sensible but stylish heels clicked smartly. "I know a tailor three blocks away who can have your dress uniform ready in one day. After your fitting, we'll compose a five-minute speech that you can use for your first three appearances. That speech will be your new best friend. It will become as familiar to you as the pledge of allegiance, and you won't need to use note cards. You're going to want to keep eye contact with your audience."

She could barely contain her delight—any job in the State Department! Offers from Congress! The top general of the country guaranteeing her future! She might end up with an office above ground and, maybe-just-maybe-oh-maybe, a window! She had no doubt that this was the kind of moment that came just once in a career. It certainly had never happened before.

The excitement of the assignment accounted for her skittering heartbeat and quickened breath.

She was so thrilled with her good fortune and so touched by his plight that she had nearly—but not quite—forgiven him for his boorish behavior. Probably had gotten flustered at the sight of a female—although his kiss had all the confidence of a conqueror taking his due.

Flustered, that's it, she thought.

The darker prospect, that he was a natural-born jerk, she did her best to ignore.

Still, if they were going to spend the next thirty days together and if she was going to make a career move on her success transforming him into a gentleman, she'd have to let go of her indignation.

She wouldn't even tell him that she could have done without the Girl Scout comment, that she had enjoyed being a Girl Scout and she didn't see what was wrong with them.

"We'll sit you down with a table arrangement," she continued, balancing the schedule folder, calendar and her briefcase as she walked. "Even if you ordinarily are the sort of man who requires a seven-piece place setting with every meal, I'm sure you could use a refresher on manners. Conditions at the Baghdad prison were primitive, I've heard. By the way, I wanted to tell you that I saw you on television as you were taken to the Wiesbaden military hospital and, literally, I felt tears of pride welling up in my eyes. You really prove that Americans can overcome any...hey, where'd you go?"

She whirled around to see...nothing.

Nothing but an empty hallway that stretched the length of two city blocks. The State Department was big, with a total of twelve acres of office space spread out over eight floors.

If he had taken a wrong turn, it could take her hours to find him!

"Lieutenant McKenna?" she asked. "This way. I'm over here! Lieutenant? Lieutenant?"

Master of escape.

That's what the news had called him, noting that after months of planning and several failed attempts, McKenna had slipped all thirty-two of his men out of the jail without a trace and had even gotten a day's lead on the manhunt that followed.

He hadn't taken a wrong turn—he had given her the slip.

But the corridors of Washington office buildings were Chessey's home turf, and she had an advantage. She stilled. And listened. And shook her head.

The telltale echo of cowboy boots treading on stone-cold government-issue linoleum.

"Lieutenant McKenna, you get back here right now!" she exclaimed, trotting down the hall at the fullest speed possible in her heels. She ignored the shocked stare of a secretary coming from the opposite direction. She knew, she knew...as a Banks Bailey she was ordinarily so dignified.

But dignity shmignity, that man was her future! Without him, she'd be stuck in a basement closet of an office until she reached the age of retirement! Without him, Winston Fairchild III would never look at her again and he'd certainly never bring his suitable self to the Banks Bailey compound for holidays. She'd still be the black sheep of the Banks Baileys, without the approval and respect of her family. This job, this lieutenant, this assignment meant a lot.

"Lieutenant McKenna, you're not leaving! We have work to do."

She ran down the stairwell at top speed. With a half-dozen frantic excuse me's, she pushed her way through a crowd of schoolchildren and their chaperones gathered in the Diplomatic Lobby.

Out on Twenty-third Street, she looked left and right.

And then she saw him.

"Lieutenant McKenna, I said we have work to do!"

She trotted after him, regretting her heels, desperate not to lose him as a Japanese tourist group clogged the sidewalk. He walked away with no more regard for her frantic shouts than he did for any other street distraction. The cabdriver leaning on his horn and bellowing at the driver in front of him. The jackhammer grinding cement on the next corner. The youth with a boom box playing heavy metal.

Still, he was not the type she could lose in a crowd. He stood out—taller than anyone on the street. He wore a pair of worn-out jeans that fit low on his hips and a button-down shirt that showed the wrinkles of a twelve-hour transatlantic flight. It was white—the kind of white that reflects that dazzling sun. He had a muscular build, surprising given his time in prison, but Chessey remembered reading somewhere that he had required all his men to maintain absolutely peak physical conditioning. And had required nothing less from himself. His hair was cut a little longer than regulation. His skin was ruddy and sunburned, which only accentuated his blue eyes.

He garnered his share of second looks from women in his path, but not a flicker of recognition since, courtesy of an Army shave and a haircut, he bore little resemblance to the ragged hero who had led his men to the Turkish border.

"Derek McKenna, you stop right there!" Chessey shrieked, grabbing his elbow as he came to a stop at the crosswalk.

He glanced at her with a sorrowful expression that made her back off. Made her think, right then, right there, that maybe it was cruel to take a man like this and parade him around the country for a month. But then he followed his haunted-eye look with something approaching a leer and then pride-smashing dismissal.

"I'm not going with you," he said. "Save your animal-training tricks for some other sucker."

"They'll call the President."

He tilted his chin thoughtfully. For a scant second, as the sun played across his face, Chessey thought she saw warmth and longing in his eyes. On the other hand, it could have simply been glare.

"I've been giving the President some thought. I don't think he will reinstate me. He can't afford the bad publicity. So I'm going to do what I've wanted to do since the moment I got captured by the Iraqis. I'm going home."

The light changed. He stepped forward. She held her ground in front of him. He took another step, invading her space with the natural scent of bay leaf and musk. She tilted her chin up, balanced on her toes, rued the fact that even with her heels he was a good six inches taller than she was. It was hard to look like an authority figure when she could hardly keep her balance and she still had to look up at him.

His mouth was scant inches from her, his sweet minty breath a whisper at her forehead. She wondered if he was going to kiss her again.

She wondered what she would do if he did.

"You have a problem with me going home?"

"I do. What about the enlisted men?" she asked, remembering how he had been thrown off balance by the general with just the same concern.

His eyes narrowed.

"What about 'em?"

"Their morale."

"If the men don't know that their officers will stick by them, then the military's got a bigger problem on its hands than I could ever solve in a month of stump speeches."

"You can't go!"

She didn't realize until he looked at his chest that her fingers, perfectly manicured in ballet slipper pink, were splayed along the rock-hard definition of his chest muscles.

"Darlin', I didn't know my kiss could affect you like this," he drawled.

She jerked as if he were a hot stove. He reached to the sidewalk and handed her the schedule she had dropped. He lingered a nanosecond at her long legs.

"I'm just trying to do my job," she said stiffly. "It's nothing personal."

He stood up.

"Then you'll understand that it's nothing personal, but I'm going home."

He stepped around her and walked across the street.

"But you're a hero!" she cried, scrambling to keep up with him.

"I'm done with this hero business. Want nothing more to do with it."

He held his hand straight in the air. A cab screeched to a halt in front of him.

"Where are you going?" Chessey demanded.

"The airport. It's faster than walking to Kentucky."

"I'm going with you."

"Oh, I don't think so," he said, getting into the cab. "My pappy told me a long time ago that any woman I brought home with me had better be bride material."

In a split second pondering the gray, sunless office she called her own and the sense of personal failure that was her constant companion, Chessey decided she didn't care what a man named Pappy said.

She opened the cab door, took advantage of the lieutenant's reflexive good manners by nudging him over to give her room and told the cabdriver to take them both to Dulles Airport.

"Here you are, sir," the ticket agent said, handing McKenna a ticket envelope. She tilted her face to the side and smiled winningly. "One-way to Louisville, Kentucky, connecting with the commuter flight to the Elizabethtown airfield. Have a nice trip, sir."

"Thanks," McKenna said, fingering the envelope reverently. Home. He was finally going home. He grinned, knowing the ticket agent misinterpreted his expression as interest in her but being powerless to stop himself. "Thanks, ma'am."

She blushed.

And then the protocol specialist shoved her way past him, throwing her briefcase on the counter.

"I'll have what he's having," Chessey said.

"Oh," said the ticket agent. "Are you two together?"

"No," Derek said.

"Yes," Chessey said.

"No."

"Yes."

"No."

"This is a free country!"

"We've already discussed freedom in the cab," Derek said impatiently. "I'm going home. You're not going with me. A free country means I don't have to be with you.''

''A free country means I can go anywhere I want,'' Chessey corrected. ''Miss, I'll be going with him. Wherever he's going.''

The ticket agent's magenta nails poised above her computer keys.

''Sir?''

''Don't give her a ticket. I don't want her going with me.''

''You can't tell her what to do.''

''Ma'am?'' He pleaded.

''I want to go with him!'' Chessey wailed.

Derek shook his head. Considering this woman was a maximum of five-five and had less than half his weight on her frame, she wasn't intimidated and certainly didn't back down.

The third man in the line waiting to buy tickets harrumphed.

''If she loves you and is willing to make a go of it, you should give it another chance, young man,'' he offered. ''Too many young people think that they can just walk out on marriages without—''

''I'm not married to her!'' Derek roared. ''She's a protocol specialist at the State Department who's aching to make a promotion on baby-sitting me for a month. She followed me in a cab and talked my ear off all the way here about duty to my country and freedom meaning that she could go anywhere I went.''

For emphasis, he jabbed his fingers in Chessey's direction and wasn't comforted by her smile.

On any other woman it would have been a come-on, but on this protocol specialist he figured it was pure trouble.

''Why, Lieutenant Derek McKenna,'' she said, slowly and carefully enunciating every syllable of his name. And she added for the benefit of the few people in the line who didn't immediately do a double take, ''Derek McKenna. It must be the stress of being a hero that's making you act so erratically. You need rest. And some reassurance that America loves you. Oh, Lieutenant Derek McKenna, we all think you're wonderful!''

''Derek McKenna?'' The woman behind Chessey repeated.

''Derek McKenna,'' Chessey confirmed.

The woman stared. Derek felt a queasy feeling in his stomach as he watched her dawning recognition.

''Derek McKenna!'' she shrieked. ''I'm so delighted to meet you. Could I get your autograph?''

As the woman yanked apart her carry-on luggage to find something to write with, the man who had given him a lecture on marital behavior pumped his hand.

"Just shaking hands with you is a privilege," he said.

The rope-cordoned line surged toward Derek, with requests for autographs, kisses, pictures and handshakes running pretty much even. Derek craned to catch Chessey's eye, to give her some indication that he held her directly responsible for this calamity or at least to make her feel miserable about herself—as she should! But Chessey coolly turned her back on him and pulled out her employee ID card.

"State Department, official business," she said briskly, holding her ID out to the ticket agent. "I need a spot on the plane next to him."

"One way or round trip?"

"Actually, let's start talking flights from Elizabethtown to New York three days from now."

The ticket agent peered at the ID, little realizing that it only entitled Chessey to entry into her office building in the morning and an employee discount at the cafeteria for lunch.

"Right away, ma'am. Is that really Derek McKenna?"

"Sure is."

"Wow. Totally cool."

After concluding her business with the ticket agent, Chessey decided it was time to rescue the lieutenant from his adoring public. But as she made her way through the crowd surrounding him, she realized he was doing just great on his own. He juggled a baby girl in one arm as her proud parents snapped Polaroids. He listened patiently to a grouch tell him how the military was better in his day. He endured with a winning smile a kiss on the cheek from a giggling teen—and her mother— and didn't even follow up with an inappropriate leer like the one he had given Chessey at Winston's office.

"Sorry, folks, I'm having a great time meetin' you all," he said, jerking a finger at Chessey. "But Ms. Bailey Banks from the State Department—"

"Chessey Banks Bailey," Chessey corrected.

"Banks Bailey. Whoever she is, she's got my time filled. You know, official stuff. Government stuff. You can understand, folks."

Although the crowd lingered, clearly wanting some of the gold dust of heroism to rub off on them, Chessey and Derek drifted away.

"Thanks for getting me out of—" Derek said, and he suddenly jerked his head. "Hey, wait a minute, you got me into that. I'm not thanking you for anything."

"You were wonderful," Chessey said, deciding that she would use with him the same positive reinforcement methods used by kindergarten teachers everywhere. "You're a natural with people."

"And you're going to try to change that."

"Not at all. I just want to smooth out some rough edges."

"Well, too bad. Because I'm going home, and in my part of the country, they don't care if a man has rough edges."

He turned.

"Why are you following me?"

"Because I've got a ticket for the same flight to Louisville. And the connecting flight to Elizabethtown."

"It's E'town. You don't pronounce the *L*, the *I*, the *Z*, the *A*, the *B*, the *E*, the *T* or the *H*. And don't bother coming, because my pappy's going to pick me up at the airfield, and there won't be room in the pickup for you."

"I'll take a cab."

"E'town doesn't have any cabs."

"I'll hitchhike."

"Dangerous thing for a woman alone to do."

"I'll walk."

He threw up his hands in frustration.

"Good luck to you then, because those high heels aren't going to get you more than a mile outside the airport. And I'll be long gone by then."

"He's determined to go home," Chessey said into the phone, craning her neck to keep an eye on Derek, who was standing in line at the snack concession.

"It's your job to get him to New York in time for the luncheon," Winston said impatiently. "But if you want to throw in the towel now, I'll get someone else working on it."

Chessey thought of her promotion and of Winston and of what both things meant to her.

"I'll get him to New York. I'm just telling you where we'll be until then."

"Hero's homecoming."

"Huh?"

"Too bad we can't get this on national news," Winston said. "Hero's homecoming. But I know I'm not going to be able to persuade any of the networks or even CNN to cover this. Why couldn't his hometown be Beverly Hills or Palm Beach?"

She was about to say that he wouldn't be the kind of man he was if he had been raised in the playgrounds of the rich and pampered, but she realized Winston would take that as an indictment of the way he had been brought up.

The way she would have been brought up if she weren't from the side of the Banks Bailey family that was considered trouble.

"Who's picking you up at the airport?"

"His pappy," Chessey replied.

"Pappy?" Winston said, with the same intonation one might reserve for raw squid served up as an appetizer. "Well, it does have a certain Americana feel to it. I suppose he's the one with the farm.''

''Yes.''

''It's in a town called Brownsville?''

''Yes.''

''And your ETA in Elizabethtown is four o'clock?''

''It's E'town. You don't pronounce the *L*, the *I*, the *Z*, the *A*, the *B*, the *E*, the *T* or the *H*.''

''You and the general. You're both turning into hicks. Next you'll be wearing overalls and chewing on grass stalks. Get McKenna to New York in presentable fashion.''

''You can count on me,'' she said, but Winston had already hung up.

She walked to the snack bar and sat at the booth across from Derek. On the table in front of him was a red plastic tray. On the tray were six hot dogs, each piled high with mustard, ketchup, onions, tomatoes, relish, pickles and hot peppers. He slurped down a soda, this time mercifully choosing to drink from the can in the ordinary manner.

''No, you're not sitting with me,'' he said, motioning her away. ''I want to eat in peace.''

''You're going to eat all of those?''

''Every last one of them,'' Derek said proudly. ''There were a lot of things I missed in prison, and American-style hot dogs were one of them. Now, skedaddle to another table. I don't want you working your persuasive charm on me or telling me the proper method for eating these. And I'm not going anywhere with you.''

''Why, Lieutenant—''

His hand clamped over her mouth with lightning speed. His callused hands made the touch seem brutal, and he immediately recognized that, muttering an apology even as he issued his warning.

''Don't do that to me again.''

He picked up a hot dog.

''Oh, all right, stop looking at me with those big baby blue eyes,'' he said. ''I'm not going to hurt you. You can sit with me, but don't talk to me.''

''Thank—''

''All right, all right, don't say anything. Just don't talk to me.''

''Sure, Derek,'' she said, zipping her fingers across her lips. ''Not a word out of me.''

His eyes narrowed. He's suspicious, Chessey thought, taking a potato chip from his tray so that he'd know that she wouldn't speak—absolutely not with her mouth full.

He glanced around the airport, double-taking a woman in a tight blue miniskirt. Chessey smiled. Let him look. Let him get distracted. Let him forget his suspicions as his head swiveled to catch sight of an attractive woman walking in the opposite direction.

Let him put his guard down.

Because while she wasn't sure she could have survived ten minutes in the Baghdad jail and she was certain she couldn't have managed the escape to the Turkish border, she was positive that she was stronger than the lieutenant in one respect.

She wasn't letting go of him until she had her promotion—until she had the job that would do the Banks Bailey name proud.

Chapter Three

She didn't talk to him as he downed five hot dogs in rapid succession—didn't even express her revulsion at all that fat and empty calories. Only nodded in mute gratitude when he passed the sixth hot dog to her and said she looked like she hadn't had lunch.

Chessey didn't try to tell him how important his speaking tour was when he got up to walk to the departure gate.

She didn't explain how quickly the month would speed by as they flew to Louisville.

Didn't tell him that his drinking soda from a can or popping the airline's honey roasted peanuts in the air and catching them with his mouth embarrassed her and was definitely inappropriate.

She even affected silent indifference when the flight attendant gave him her phone number.

They hit turbulence in the green mountains near E'town, but she didn't say a word.

It was probably the longest period of time she had gone without talking in her whole life.

But when they got off the plane at E'town airfield, she couldn't help herself. It was time to speak.

He hadn't lied to her.

Hadn't misled her one little bit.

But Chessey had simply assumed he was wrong about their destination—or perhaps the long imprisonment had made his memory faulty.

How could an airport exist without a taxi stand?

She looked around for a spot of yellow or white-and-black checks on the horizon and found...none.

How could an airport be built that didn't have shuttle buses to everywhere in a fifty-mile radius?

She pulled out her tortoise-framed sunglasses and stared.

Or at least a bank of telephones and an information desk?

She looked behind her, in front of her and to each side. No helpful signs telling the traveler where to go for his or her needs.

How could an airport be nothing more than a rusting corrugated steel hangar and a strip of red clay runway in a clearing between trees and more trees?

"Welcome to E'town," the pilot said, handing Chessey her briefcase.

Hey, wait a minute, Derek McKenna was leaving!

"Goodbye, Miss Banks Bailey," Derek said.

And it was at that moment that she broke her silence.

"You're not leaving me here, are you?"

The four-seater prop plane they had arrived in was already taking on passengers for its turnaround. Derek strode through the grass toward a red pickup truck parked at the tree line beyond the runway.

"Take that next flight out," he called over his shoulder. He hiked up his duffel bag, which he had recovered from a storage locker at Dulles Airport. "I said goodbye and I meant it, Chessey Bailey Banks."

"It's Banks Bailey," she corrected absently, feeling the day's weary challenges catch up to her.

She watched him embrace the old man who stepped out of the driver's side of the truck. She was hot, her hair was plastered against her neck with sweat and the coppery grit that had seeped into the prop plane. Her suit was wrinkled. Her heels were slowly sinking into the wet grass. And she would have traded her grandmother's black

South Seas pearls around her neck for a nice, cold glass of water.

A hundred yards out of reach, Derek threw his duffel into the back of the truck and got in. The truck peeled out onto the blacktop road.

"Ma'am, the gentleman said somethin' 'bout you heading back," drawled the pilot. "I can't get you on this flight 'cuz I got passengers to fill this run. But I can swing back this evenin' if'n you want. Just buy a ticket from the agent there. Ma'am, did you hear me?"

The lieutenant was gone. She could barely believe it, but when the truck became a red dot and the red dot became nothing, she was forced to acknowledge the truth. Derek McKenna had slipped—make that strode—through her fingers, taking with him her once-in-a-career, once-in-a-lifetime opportunity.

She squared her shoulders. She wasn't descended from the *Mayflower*'s Banks Bailey family for nothing.

"And who is the ticket agent?" she asked.

"Rumsey Houchin, right over there. You want me to wait?"

"No, absolutely not," she said firmly.

She followed the pilot's pointed finger to a man in a sweat- and oil-stained coverall who disappeared into the hangar. She thanked the pilot, who latched shut the cabin door. As he settled into his seat, he gave her a friendly thumbs-up and then taxied down the clay runway. The prop plane stumbled into the skies, taking with it all hope of a strategic retreat to Washington.

She entered the hangar, assuming correctly that she did not need to knock. She strode past skeletons of single-engine Cessnas and half-assembled props to find a pair of denim-covered legs sticking out of the hood of a red Corvette.

"Pardon me, but would you happen to know the location of the Pappy McKenna farm?"

A red face jerked out from under the hood and scrutinized her top to toe to top again.

"You came with Derek?"

"Yes, I did."

"I heard he was back in the States," Rumsey said, rubbing a dark oil slick across the front of his coverall. He extended his hand but reconsidered when he saw her recoil. "Folks 'round here never believed he was dead—the good Lord's never made a jam that Derek McKenna can't get himself out of. You fixin' on marrying?"

"No."

"Pappy don't want Derek bringing home women he don't intend on making honest," Rumsey brayed, shoving his head under the hood.

"Please, Mr. Houchin, I would like to pay you to drive me to the McKenna farm."

He looked at her again.

"You love him?"

"Of course not."

"Pregnant?"

"No. It's a strictly professional relationship."

A sharp intake of breath and a grunt that mingled shock and horror.

"Mr. Houchin? Are you all right?"

"I'm sorry, but you just look too pretty and fresh like to be that kind of woman. But I guess it takes all kinds."

"I'm from the State Department!" Chessey cried, outraged, as she finally understood his point. "I'd like to call a taxi."

The murmur from the car engine seemed to say "taxis are for city folks," but might just have meant "faxes won't deliver yolks."

Chessey tried again.

"Would you drive me to the McKenna farm?"

The response was clear.

"Nope."

"Then at least tell me where the farm is."

Rumsey pulled his head out.

"All right, I guess I can do you that much. You need to get onto Route 65. It's yonder up that way," he said, pointing toward the clock that advertised a local brewery. "Five, maybe ten miles. Get yourself to Cave City and then head up 70 to Brownsville." He pointed to a Cessna skeleton on the other side of the hangar. "When you get to the gas station at Brownsville, go right on the fork in the road.'' He pointed to a screen door.

''And how far is it?''

Rumsey Houchin scratched the back of his head with a wrench.

''Not too sure. I don't get out there much. Maybe fifty miles. Make that sixty. No. Can't be that far. I guess I don't rightly know because the mountain roads are pretty twisty.''

Chessey shook her head. Fifty, sixty, twisty roads. There wasn't much difference. She'd never make it in these heels.

''I have a one-hundred-dollar bill in my brief-case. You drive me to the farm and it's yours.''

He rattled his wrench at her.

''Keep your money. I ain't setting Pappy off.''

''I have to get to the farm,'' she said. ''It's important government business.''

''Now, miss, don't you think that boy's had enough of government business?''

Rumsey shoved his head under the hood of the Corvette.

''Please,'' she pleaded.

''Either buy a ticket for the next flight out or get the hell out of my hangar,'' Rumsey said from under the hood. ''I won't have nobody bothering Derek McKenna with my help.''

After a couple of minutes of watching Mr.

Houchin energetically working on the car, Chessey gave up.

All right, if she had to she'd walk.

She paused to review her directions on the cement steps leading out of the front door of the hangar. The heaven-grazing trees dripped voluptuous green leaves, the setting sun filtered through fluffy pink and orange clouds, and the cicadas squealed their summer sonata.

It was actually quite a beautiful place, a natural setting that could take a woman's breath away. A spectacular vista for a woman who had been cooped up too much of her life with skyscrapers, sidewalks and taxicabs on every corner.

But Chessey wasn't in the mood for *National Geographic* style rhapsodies on the beauty of nature. She sized up the convoluted ribbon of road. She'd have to hitch a ride. Best way to do it would be to get on Route 65. If she met anybody along the way, she still had money in her briefcase and enough sense to avoid discussions of matrimony.

She walked. Ignoring the persistent blister on her right heel. Slapping a mosquito attracted to her perfume. Shifting her briefcase from hand to hand as it grew heavier.

She didn't think anything of the first drop of water.

Instead, she was wondering if she could fax Derek's measurements to her tailor in Washington and then have his uniform overnighted to catch up with them in New York.

Or the second drop.

She shifted her briefcase to her other hand and was grateful that she had always been the type to put in it her wallet, a cosmetic bag, her toothbrush and an extra set of underwear in a Ziploc bag in the inner pocket. This Girl Scout came prepared.

Or the third drop.

She could ask her cousin Merriweather to loan her the keys to her New York apartment so she could freshen up before the Council of Aeronautics luncheon.

She was actually feeling quite optimistic, making plans and contingency plans and backup plans to the contingency plans when the fluffy clouds turned black, the trees flipped their leaves and the heavens opened up with a torrent.

"No," she said.

But the sky didn't listen.

"No," she repeated.

And then she matched the skies, raindrop for raindrop, tear for tear, sob for cloud-battering sob.

Her heels sank completely into the clay and mud ditch. Her jacket dripped water off its braided hem. Strands of soaked blond hair stuck to her cheeks.

Eyes squeezed shut in a miserable attempt to get a grip on herself, she didn't see the red pickup truck driving toward her. Didn't hear it pull a

U-turn so tight that its passenger door ended up directly parallel to her. Didn't open her eyes until he shoved his head out the window and told her to get in.

"Don't you have sense enough to stay out of the rain?" he demanded.

She was so overjoyed, so happy to see Derek that she didn't argue, didn't let loose with any comeback that he certainly would have deserved. He cranked the door open and she regarded the dry cab of the truck as if it were paradise.

He slid over next to the driver, a short, grizzled man in overalls who grunted a hello, ma'am. She closed the door as the pickup lurched forward.

"Pappy, I'm not bringing her here because I want to," Derek said. "This is not a getting-married kind of thing."

"Good thing," Pappy said, hazarding one glance at Chessey. She self-consciously finger combed her hair from her face. "Good thing you're not getting married."

"Oh, really?" Chessey asked.

"You're too much alike to be locked in holy matrimony. Pigheaded, that's what you both are."

Derek looked at Chessey and she could read his thoughts as surely as if he spoke aloud.

Pigheaded—okay, I can accept that. But I'm like her?

Chessey pursed her lips and stared back.

Pigheaded—in Washington, we call that assertive and it's a good thing. But like him?

No way, they agreed with silent, nearly imperceptible shakes of their heads.

It was the only thing they agreed on that day.

Cave City, Renfrow Market, Pig-Pen Junction, Shotgun, Brownsville.

The little towns that dotted the drive to the McKenna farm were nothing more than ma-and-pa grocery stores and an occasional tourist come-on in the form of rocks lined up on an entrepreneur's fence post. All rocks—two dollars would buy a nice one—were guaranteed to be genuine from Mammoth Caves and were irresistible to the occasional traveler who lost his way on the nicely paved, four-lane Interstate 65 twenty miles east that deposited tourists at Mammoth Cave National Park's front entrance.

Although the interstate would have taken a good half-hour off their travel time, Pappy and Derek had their own way of going home. It was old-fashioned but it worked. And they didn't have to read billboards.

Spaced between the towns were tobacco, soy and dairy farms and their farmhouses. Sagging barns and steel silos. Fields wet and green. Dairy cows being brought in out of the rain by children with horsetail switches.

Chessey noticed it was a poor land. The houses were small, one story and brick. An occasional carpenter Gothic. The folks sitting in their front porch swings didn't wear fancy clothes. The grocery stores advertised soda pops for fifty cents a can. And Pappy had to negotiate a road that occasionally ran to copper clay.

But Derek only cared he was home, and the sweet, pungent scent of farm dirt filled his lungs. He looked at the woman. Her hair was pulled from her forehead in a tight, sleek bun. She was working on her pink lipstick in the passenger side mirror—how she managed it when Pappy was driving over gravel, dirt, rock and blacktop!

He smiled lazily. She didn't like this place, couldn't like this place, wouldn't last a minute…and a minute of careful planning was a lot less than thirty days of road torture.

Derek was a thinker, a planner, naturally gifted at figuring out the escape route.

And he knew it.

A minute was all he needed to work this one out.

It was only his weakness for a woman in distress that had made him get Pappy to turn around and save her as the rain started because he knew, just knew, she would try to walk.

But that didn't mean he would let her stay.

He wanted her to go back to Washington and

leave him to the rest of his peaceful, inactive, rest-and-work life. She had to go willingly on the next day's flight out of E'town. She had to want it.

"Pappy, let's stop at Nona's."

"I got dinner at home."

"No, I want some souse."

Pappy recoiled.

"You never liked souse," he said dismissively. "That's my kind of food. The kind of food folks ate in the Depression."

"Well, I've missed it."

"Souse? Nobody misses souse. Least of all you."

"What's souse?" Chessey asked, brushing the last water drops off her skirt. Derek did a double take. With the addition of lipstick and a spritz of clean scent at her earlobes, she looked as fresh and as perfect as she had when she walked into the State Department office and he had kissed her.

"What's souse?" Chessey asked again, breaking his momentary daydream about the feel of her lips against his.

He cleared his throat.

Stay focused, he commanded himself.

"Souse is a little specialty of this part of Kentucky," he said. "When I was in Baghdad, I really got the cravings for it."

Pappy harrumphed.

"Son, there's twenty things I could list off that

you'd develop a craving for, and souse ain't one of them.''

Nonetheless Pappy pulled off into a muddy ditch in front of the Winona Market just as the rain stilled. Chessey opened the passenger door, took a long look at the gravel, copper and clay muck and closed it again. Derek didn't budge.

"I was going to get out on your side," he said with what he hoped was his most innocent smile. "Ladies first."

She looked down again, then looked at the open driver's side door, which Pappy had just exited, and looked at Derek. He willed himself not to move.

"Those are an awful nice pair of shoes," he observed. "Ferragamo?"

"Chanel."

"Whooee. I bet you paid a pretty penny for them. Shame if they get any more beat up than they already are."

"Yes, it would be, wouldn't it?" she said coolly.

"If it's getting to be too much for you, I can have Pappy drive you to Paducah or back to E'town," he said. "They've got plenty of nice ladies' stores. Hotels, motels, too, if you don't want to stay on our farm. Nice restaurants with the best cuisine. Of course, like we were discussing earlier, it's a free country and you can stay where you—''

She was already out of the truck, sinking rapidly but keeping her balance with a firm grip on the door handle. She lifted one leg, and as she did, her other leg began its descent into the muck.

Derek counted to twenty to stop himself from weakening to her dilemma. He waited for the request to be driven to civilization, which was sure to come.

But when he got to seventeen, she yanked her feet out of her shoes and walked barefoot to join Pappy at the porch steps to Winona's.

"Hey, these are Chanel!" Derek exclaimed. He scrambled out of the truck, made a one-handed grab for both shoes and shot across the gully of mud, gravel, coppery clay and rainwater.

"That's all right," she said with a whisper of a smile that would turn most men's legs to jelly. "I want to respect the local custom of going barefoot."

Two dirt-faced youngsters in overalls and T-shirts identifying their heavy metal band preferences came onto the porch. They had bare feet— what child would wear shoes willingly in summer? Derek dropped the Chanels. Out of the corner of his eye, he saw Pappy shaking his head.

"Pigheaded," Pappy snapped. "You two are so danged pigheaded."

He swung open the wood screen door and went in.

"Well, that's what souse is," Derek said to Chessey.

"Pig heads?" Chessey said, with a telltale intake of breath.

"Yes, ma'am," he replied, opening the door for her with a flourish. "Souse is pig brains, intestines and other internal organs suspended in a gelatin-like goo."

"Aspic," she said. "The gelatin would be aspic."

"Yeah, I guess that's what your kind would call it. Round here we eat it with crackers, cheese and Tabasco sauce. Wash it down with a cola. Are you coming?"

The children looked at Chessey as if she were an alien. And she might as well be—perfectly coiffed and manicured and dressed from her knees up. Down from her knees, though, Derek saw wretched runs in her stockings, streaks of rust-colored mud oozing from between her toes.

Still, mighty nice legs, he noted.

"Are you getting married, Derek?" one of the children asked. "'Cause I heard your pappy don't want you bringing women around."

"No!" Derek shoved Chessey ahead of him into Winona's.

In the instant the screen door slammed shut, he

felt the ache of homesickness satisfied, an aching that he hadn't known was more than a mere craving for the safety of his men. The smell of corn hush puppies frying, the red-and-white vinyl wallpaper shiny with grease and the creak of the floorboards as Winona lumbered toward him.

"Derek McKenna, my little baby!" A white-haired woman, her girth straining against a denim housedress, flung her arms around his waist. "My little little little baby."

Out of the corner of his eye, he saw Chessey's bemusement.

He frowned.

"Here, Winona, gotcha a little something," he said, untangling her arms. He reached into his jeans pocket and handed her a small crystal bottle.

"Bal a Versailles!" Winona shrieked. "You remembered!"

"I never forget my first girlfriend."

"Every time he comes home he brings me this," Winona explained to Chessey. "I can't get it around here and I was just about running out. I bet you didn't bring this back from Baghdad."

"Washington," Derek said.

"Is that where you got this one?" Winona asked, inspecting Chessey.

"Yes."

"Don't she need a pair of shoes?"

"She's into local customs."

"Only children go off without their shoes," Winona said.

"I think she won't be happy here."

"When's the wedding?"

Pappy came out from behind the first and only aisle carrying a can of Tabasco sauce, a box of saltines and a six-pack of cola in bottles.

"They're not getting married," he said.

"Well, then, what are you here for?" Winona asked Chessey.

"Souse. Derek said he wanted some souse. And I understand you make the best. I've been looking forward to it for the last half mile."

Flattery. Pure flattery. Delivered with a smile. Derek could see it plain as day. He could resist it.

But Winona couldn't. No, no, Winona sighed with pleasure, put her perfume in her pocket and went in back of the deli counter. She pulled out a slab of clear-wrapped souse and laid it out for Chessey's inspection. The clear gelatin casing was punctuated with ground-up bits of meat.

Derek felt a familiar queasiness.

"Looks wonderful," Chessey said. "Derek said this is served with cheese, crackers and Tabasco sauce. I would love to try some. With a cola, please."

Winona gave one narrow-eyed indication that she knew Derek couldn't be up to no good. Then she turned her attention to creating a plate of souse.

She slapped Pappy's hands away several times as he reached to grab extra slices. Chessey scooped one cracker into her hand and bit in. She closed her eyes as if swept away with pleasure.

Darn! She actually ate it! And then asked for seconds!

It was impossible to scare this woman off!

"Derek, here's some for you," Winona offered.

He looked at Chessey. Why wasn't she turning up her nose? Why wasn't she revolted by this? Why wasn't she asking for a return trip out of E'town?

He took the cracker. Looked at the souse and cheese. The Tabasco sauce was about to drip. He had to do it. He brought it to his open mouth.

He thought about the little pig he had raised as a pet when he was a kid.

The next thing he knew he was standing on the front porch of the grocery store, breathing deeply and gratefully of the moist, grassy air. He leaned on the porch railing.

The screen door squealed open.

"Lieutenant, I appreciate your effort."

He turned. She carried nothing more lethal than a bottle of cola, which she handed to him.

"You do?"

"Yes. But you aren't going to succeed at scaring me off. I'm going to do my job, and you're going to do yours. And when I'm through, you're going to be as at ease in boardrooms, television studios and hotel ballrooms as I looked like I was in there. That's all that etiquette is about, and that's what I do for a living.''

He wiped his mouth as if a sour taste had developed.

''And you're going to do it for thirty days,'' Chessey added.

''Oh, no. Not me. I'm satisfied with what I am and I'm not changing a thing,'' he said, jabbing a finger at her. ''Tomorrow morning, you're getting on the first flight out of E'town. Alone.''

Chapter Four

The McKennas owned a ten-acre farm presided over by a white clapboard farmhouse and a red barn, both built by Pappy's grandpa when he had traded potato farming in Ireland for tobacco farming in America. Pappy's father had forsaken tobacco for dairy cows, and Pappy had shifted the farm to soy when that crop proved more profitable. Regardless of the crop, the McKenna men had a way with the earth, with the cycles of nature's bounty.

The McKenna talent had stopped with Derek, who had fled for the life of adventure ten years before. Oh, he could work a farm like his father, worked hard at it, too. Derek could drive a tractor by ten, plan irrigation lines by twelve and by fifteen could keep the books. But his soul wasn't in it. College couldn't satisfy his hunger to experience the world, and he had enlisted to escape the boredom, the early-to-bed-early-to-rise life-style, the isolation of farm life.

And though he loved his pappy dearly, he regarded his leaves as duty runs. A bottle of Bal a Versailles for Winona, flowers for the grave of the mother who had died while he was an infant, a week of taking over his father's chores, a trip to the veterans' nursing home and he was only too glad to go back to base.

Or at least, he and everyone who knew him thought the gift for farming had ended with Derek. But as he drove the pickup down the muddy drive, it was all he could do not to step on the brake, climb out of the driver's seat and kiss the soil.

He was home.

Home was a word that settled in a man's stomach and tugged down hard so that his breath was caught and his voice quivered. It was a word that jumbled a man's brain, making poetry out of gruff talk and masterpiece paintings out of something that had once looked like a collection of lumber, nails, soil and John Deere equipment.

He had come home. Home for him was this farm, and he would worship it as his father and grandfather and great-grandfather before him. He was a farmer. Yes, he was a farmer.

"Pappy?"

"I know, son. You ain't ever leaving again, is that it?"

"No, I ain't never goin' nowhere," Derek said, noticing that the contradictory rhythms and rhymes of Kentucky talk had come back to him as easily as the rumored ability to ride bicycles comes to others.

A blond head peered over Pappy's shoulder.

"I hate to burst your bubble, Lieutenant, but you're due in New York in three days."

"Dang! I nearly forgot you were here," Derek said. "Squeezed in like that against the window and not having given me the free country lecture for ten whole minutes."

"I'm still here, and I'm escorting you to New York. And then on to Baltimore."

"Miss Bailey Banks Banks Bailey or whatever," he said, waving away her correction. "I am not going anywhere with you. 'Cepting possibly the E'town airfield tomorrow morning."

"You've made an agreement with the government," she said primly over his father's shoulder. "The head of the Joint Chiefs of Staff is expecting you to honor that agreement."

"I'm sorry to disappoint you and the general— I'll even call him myself if it makes you feel better. But I'm staying home. And you're leaving. I only made Pappy here turn around and drive back for you because I'm the kind of man who can't let stray dogs suffer.''

Her outrage was swift and potent. With a niggling sense of being catapulted into the emotional territory of third grade, Derek got a kick out of the pop of color on her cheeks and the fire in her sapphire eyes.

"I am no stray dog! I am an assistant protocol specialist for the United States—"

"Kids!" Pappy yelled, elbowing the combatants for room. "Could you stop interfering with the magic of having my one and only child return home after most sane folks had given him up for dead?"

"Sorry, Mr. McKenna," Chessey mumbled.

"Sorry, Pappy."

"Just drive the car, son. Nice and slow, savor everything you've been missing, a silent meditation on the wonders of nature and the bounty of the good Lord for helping you find your way home.''

Derek had always thought there were two kinds of men in the world—those who wink at women and those who don't need to. He had always considered himself one of the latter, but he tried out the long-forgotten skill on Chessey. Just for fun. She pursed her lips together. He got such a kick out of it he nearly didn't hear Pappy.

"Then you'll want to tie up the fencing there

where the snows pulled it down.'' His father pointed as the truck passed a break in the fence. ''After that, you'll want to concentrate on the barn. Needs a good sanding, coat of paint and some new boards on the...''

The moment of silent meditation on the wonders of nature and the bounty of the good Lord was clearly over.

''Make a list,'' Derek said. ''I'll get started tomorrow morning.''

''And I'll help,'' Chessey said.

Both men stared.

''You...help?''

''Lieutenant, I'd be delighted to offer my assistance—until we're due in New York, that is.''

''This is work we're talking about, not paper shuffling and tea parties.''

He brought the truck to a halt in the gravel gully by the house. He got out and smelled deeply of the bluegrass scent. How had he ever been so stupid as to leave?

''I can help you,'' Chessey repeated, scrambling out of her door. ''I can help until we have to go.''

Derek started to argue, to point out how clearly wrong she was, to take her down a few notches and, if possible, get in a few zingers about how prissy dames like her belonged in society not on a farm. But as Pappy walked into the farmhouse, muttering, ''pigheaded,'' Derek saw just how ludicrous it was to say a word.

She was a princess, all right. Even if she was barefoot, muddy-legged and a little disheveled from travel. A princess who couldn't possibly wield a hammer, carry a two-by-four or pull a tractor in a one-eighty turn. Especially in a pink dress made by Chanel, if the double *C*s on the buttons were real.

''Fine, you can help,'' he said in surrender, feeling like an idiot when she smiled and the only thing he could think was that, if he were a lesser man, he would do whatever it took to get her to smile at him like that again.

They stood for a few awkward moments. After all, what do two combatants do when there's a momentary truce?

I want to kiss her, he thought.

Was it just this morning that he had done the same? The softness of her lips, the way her body had molded to his, the quick taste of her tongue.

He was a man and she was a woman and it had been two years in a Baghdad prison. Too long. Too long for a man with strong appetites. He raked his fingers through his close-cropped hair. He wondered if she could find him attractive. His looks, his success with women, his charm weren't anything he had ever worried about before—women had always been easy for him.

But maybe it was different now. Maybe he was different, maybe not so attractive, maybe a little rusty—make that a lot rusty—on the charm.

And maybe she was different—different from the kind of women he had known.

"Uh, Chessey," he said, thinking he should warn her this time if he was going to kiss her. And then remembering he had said he would wait until she asked, next time.

"I'll need to use your telephone," she said, pulling her briefcase from the truck. "I have to call my boss. Do you have fax capability here?"

Her magic spell was broken. She had none of the good-time charm of the kind of woman who made a one-night stand worthwhile and precious little of the gritty courage that made a farm wife.

Although she had followed him all the way here.

Then he remembered—her mission was to get him off this farm. His mission was to get her off this farm—alone.

"You can't help me," he said. "You're getting on the plane tomorrow morning. Outta here!"

He swung open the back door. He let it slap behind him without a backward glance. He sniffed fried tomatoes and chicken, cut with the sweet spice of apple pie in the oven. He looked at every knickknack—a matching sugar and flour tin set, a cookie jar with its lid broken, a clay ashtray he had made in camp—with the awe appropriate for price-

less museum treasures, if he were the sort of man
to while away his time in museums. He listened
for the lurching rhythm of the washing machine in
the basement and the news radio program Pappy
left on day and night for company. It would sound
like a fine Wagnerian opera—if he were the sort
of man who liked opera.

"Pappy, I'm really home."

"Yes, son, I've been praying you'd be here so
many times that now that you are, I can scarcely
believe it."

Pappy turned from the stove. There were tears
coursing down his face, rivers that flowed into the
worry lines that Derek knew he himself had
caused.

"Dad, I missed you, too," Derek said.

Neither was the kind of man who hugged, so
their embrace was awkward. But heartfelt.

Out of the corner of his eye, Derek saw Chessey
enter the kitchen. She mumbled something about
using the phone and had the good sense to leave
him and his father alone.

"Chessey, that man needs to be in New York
City mighty quick," Winston Fairchild III warned.
"And could you make sure his speech includes a
mention of House bill number 3482?"

"For or against?"

"Check with me later on that. The President

hasn't made up his mind. Oh, and make sure the lieutenant's wearing a dress uniform and can manage some decent table manners. He'll be seated next to the governor's wife at the aeronautics council.''

Chessey scribbled some notes on the yellow legal pad. She had spread the contents of her briefcase on the floor rather than the bed. She had chosen the screened bedroom she had guessed was reserved for guests. The brass headboard, the handmade quilt, the lace pillows and matching curtains all contributed to a restful, welcoming atmosphere. As soon as she got some of this mud off in a shower, she was going to slip between the sheets and get some rest.

She thought of the moment of vulnerability she had seen as the lieutenant and his father hugged.

''He's pretty tired.''

''He checked out fine at the Wiesbaden military hospital,'' Winston pointed out. ''He led the men in calisthenics and weight training during their imprisonment. And he was pretty crafty at getting food and medicine for them all. He can probably make a mint on doing an exercise video when this is over.''

''He's exhausted in a different way.''

''Whatever way it is, make sure he's in New York for the aeronautics executives' lunch.''

''He needs more time!''

But Winston had left her with just a dial tone.

"Problems?"

She looked up. Derek had slipped into the room. He had showered, shaved and changed into a pair of comfortable jeans and a white oxford button-down shirt. He looked as fresh and clean as the stack of white towels he held up.

"Just the usual," she said, putting her papers and folders in her briefcase.

"You'll be in the office by tomorrow afternoon," Derek said, putting the towels on the bed. "And then you can devote your full attention to work."

"Oh, no, I'll be here," Chessey said, getting up. She didn't like the fact that he was taller than she was. Especially with her muddy pumps still in the flatbed of the truck. "I'll be taking you with me when I go to New York."

He reached out and wiped a smudge of dirt from her cheek.

She tingled at his touch and wondered if he would do more.

But he turned away, all business.

"Let's agree to disagree for tonight," he said. "Pappy sent these towels, and there's toiletries in the bathroom closet. I'm glad you figured out which one was the guest room."

She figured the gruff words were the best he

could do at saying, "Thank you for not butting in when I was hugging my dad."

"Dinner's in twenty minutes," he said, pausing at the door on his way out. "Watch out for the cottonmouths."

"Cottonmouths?"

"Oh, nothing. I shouldn't even have said anything."

"No, go ahead. What are cottonmouths?"

"No, I don't want to scare you."

"I want to hear about them," she said firmly.

"They're these snakes about—" he held his hands a foot apart and then two "—about this big. Mean bite. They live up in the Mammoth Caves, but at night they start looking for food. Nocturnal, you know. Sometimes they get in where the screen is ripped."

They both glanced casually at the windows. Just one screen was ripped at the bottom. A six-inch-long tear, hardly room for a snake. Or was it?

"Cottonmouths, huh?"

"And copperheads. You've heard of those, right?"

"Actually, no."

"Yeah, but they're nowhere near as bad as the water moccasins," Derek said. "Though you don't get too many water moccasins up this far from the river. Some, but not many. But when you do, watch out. They don't bite. They squeeze. There was a lady in Renfrow or maybe it was Brownsville when I was a child and the story is she left her baby in a crib and this water moccasin—''

"Enough," Chessey warned. "I'm on to you, Derek. You're trying to scare me with snake stories so I'll beg you to drive me to the E'town airfield. I don't scare that easy."

He touched his chest.

"Me? Scare you? I would never try such a low-down, dirty trick on you."

He had edged out of the bedroom enough so that the door could be shut on his shoulders, and that's exactly what she did.

Cottonmouths? Copperheads? Water moccasins? He was being ridiculous.

After a blissfully hot shower, Chessey changed her underwear. She found a pair of jeans and a T-shirt in the chest of drawers. The jeans were way too big, but she rolled up the hem and tied her Hermés scarf through the belt loops. The T-shirt was soft as cashmere and had Derek's name and number eleven on the back. On its front was a red horned demon twirling a basketball on an upturned trident.

"So you were a member of the Brownsville Devils," she said to her reflection in the mirror hung over the washstand. "Devils? Somehow that doesn't surprise me."

* * *

Dinner was at the white speckled-vinyl kitchen table. Fried chicken and fried tomatoes. Mashed potatoes and gravy. Pappy said grace, expressing thanks that his son had been returned to him. Apparently sensing that any conversation between Chessey and Derek would be contentious and between himself and Derek might lapse into sentimentality, Pappy very firmly kept the focus on updating Derek on gossip from the surrounding farms.

After a dessert of apple pie, Pappy announced that he was going to do the dishes and the young people should go to bed.

"If you're going to get started on that fence tomorrow morning," Pappy warned, "you need your sleep tonight."

Derek pushed his empty plate away with a satisfied sigh.

"Pappy, any other night I'd insist on helping, but I'm kind of worn-out."

"Understandable, son."

"So I'll say good-night."

He stood up, squeezed his father's shoulder and nodded a farewell to Chessey.

"Now, why don't you head off to sleep, miss?"

"I could help with dishes."

"No, let this old man have a little quiet time. I want to savor the feel of my son back home. I can do that best alone. Hope you aren't offended."

"Oh, no. Not at all."

Actually, Chessey was grateful for the opportunity to lay down after a long day.

"Besides," she added, "I've got to get started on Derek's speech."

"Won't need it!" Derek called from the hall.

"Don't start that arguing again," Pappy warned. He lowered his voice. "Miss, I know you want to take him away from me."

"I'm sorry. I hadn't thought of it that way."

"Oh, don't be making apologies. I just want a promise from you."

"Anything."

"Don't take him someplace and not send him back to me," Pappy said, and the lines on his face deepened, his good-natured smile replaced with a wistful frown. "I missed him somethin' terrible. He's all I've got."

"I'll only keep him for a month," Chessey promised. "He'll be back on this farm the day after the Fourth of July."

"Really?"

"I give you my word."

"I'll hold you to it."

Pappy turned away, saying he had a dust mote in his eye.

She discreetly said good-night, added a thank-you for his hospitality and went to the guest bedroom. From the table, she picked up a black-and-white picture in a wicker frame. A mother and baby. The mother's smile was full of love and hope. Derek's mother?

I'm going to keep my promise, Chessey thought, replacing the picture.

She stripped down to the T-shirt and her panties and got into bed with her briefcase. Outside, she heard the rising chatter of cicadas.

"I am grateful to be in New York today," she scribbled on her legal pad.

She crossed it out. Didn't sound like him. She tried again.

"I love New York."

Puh-leeze! This guy hated cities.

From a distance, she heard a dog barking.

"I stand before you a proud American."

Actually, he was a proud, nearly arrogant American all the time. Not just in New York. And certainly not just in front of aeronautics executives.

Would everyone else see the proud, and very sexual, side of this man behind the stock phrases of his speech?

She glanced at the rip in the bedroom window screen. Outside the protective glow of the nightstand lamp it was dark. Very dark.

Cottonmouths?

Absolutely not. The notion was ridiculous.

Copperheads?

As likely as Santa Claus.

Water moccasins?

She swallowed. Hard.

And nearly jumped ten feet when she heard the knock on the door. Derek stepped into the room, holding a pillow and blanket.

"My room has air-conditioning. No screen windows," he said gruffly. "Get out of here now. Before I change my mind."

Chessey pulled the sheets nearly to her neck.

"I'm doing fine."

"You're thinking about snakes."

"I'm not scared of snakes. And I'm actually quite consumed with thoughts about your upcoming speech."

"Uh-huh. Right."

"Okay, I am scared of snakes, but I don't believe your warnings about them coming in here."

"Good, because I felt too guilty to sleep," he said, turning to go.

"Wait!" Chessey cried, flinging off the sheets and jumping in front of him. It took them both just half a second to notice she had on ivory lace panties, a T-shirt and nothing else.

He gave her the once-over. Twice. Rather than cower, Chessey stared him down. He averted his eyes.

"Being from the city, I'm more used to air-conditioning," she said. "I'll sleep in your room tonight."

"Thought so."

She grabbed her pillow, briefcase and papers and wrapped his blanket around her. She retained as much composure as she would if she were wearing an evening gown to a state dinner.

"Good night, Lieutenant."

"Just a matter of air-conditioning, huh?"

She tilted her chin up.

"If you would rather that I sleep in here and you toss and turn in your bed, guilty as all get out about scaring a guest in your home with snake stories…"

"Good night," he said, shutting the door on her.

Chapter Five

By five thirty-five, Derek had to give her some credit for having spunk. Or courage. Or determination. Or maybe just what his pappy called pig-headedness.

After not much sleep—after all, was it possible for a cottonmouth to climb into a sleeping-porch screen? And did Chessey always wear white lace panties or did she sometimes wear black? Did his demons have to follow him halfway around the world?—Derek had put on a pot of coffee at five o'clock.

"No, Pappy, go on back to bed," he told his father, who had stumbled into the kitchen. He hadn't remembered his father's gait as so worn. "Pretend it's Christmas morning and sleep in."

"All right, but just till six. There's plenty of chores to be done."

Derek smiled as his father tugged at his bathrobe sash and went to his bedroom. He knew his pappy. His father wouldn't wake up until at least eleven. Sleeping in was a luxury that only a son at home afforded him. After a lifetime of hard farming, Derek figured Pappy deserved some sleeping in. He hoped his father would take advantage of it every morning.

He walked down the hall to the bedroom that had been his and tapped gently on the door. No answer. Let Miss Banks Bailey Bailey Banks sleep in, too, he thought. She was probably one of those delicate ladies who needed their beauty rest and considered waking before noon a felony.

Fine. He could use the time alone.

He put on an oilcloth jacket, since the green mountains trapped cool night air until morning sun burned it off. He took his coffee mug out to the barn, pausing to watch a deer grazing at one of the crab apple trees. As first light shot through the heavy gray-green mist, the deer bolted. He sipped at his coffee. A moment to linger over, to savor, to...

"So what's the first thing we do?"

He jerked his head and stared. That's when he told himself to give the credit she was due.

"What are you doing out of bed so early?"

She wore his T-shirt, Pappy's oil cloth, a pair of jeans rolled up at the legs and what looked to be a pair of Pappy's galoshes. Even with the ridiculously oversize getup, she still looked better than a woman had a right to this early in the morning. Clear-eyed. Her hair falling around her shoulders in soft waves. Cheerful smile, too. Was that pink lipstick she wore? She held up her coffee mug in a semi-salute.

"I'm helping, remember?"

"I don't think you'd have a clue what to do."

"Then you can teach me. And meanwhile, I'll be teaching you."

"Me?"

"Yes, I thought we'd start with forms of address," she said. "It's something you might have covered in the military, but I think you could use a refresher. And certainly, I wouldn't expect that you've had a lot of experience with meeting cardinals, senators, ambassadors and CEOs. We'll review how to address them all as we work."

"I usually call civilian women darlin', and men I try to call by their names," he said, heading for the barn. "Unless they're older than me—then I go for a respectful sir."

She tugged at his sleeve.

"I was hoping for something more sophisticated before we get to New York."

"Darlin', you keep forgetting, I'm not going to

New York. You're going back to Washington today. Alone."

He disentangled her fingers from his arm. And
as he did, he caught a glimpse of how important,
just how important, this was to her. He hated the
sorrowful look on her face, and he hated himself
for putting it there.

"All right," he conceded grudgingly. "It's a
free country. You can talk all you want. But if
you're on this farm, you gotta help out."

"I will!"

"And let me take a guess—you're not planning
on taking that flight out this morning."

"No, and I thank you in advance for your hospitality in extending an invitation to stay."

"I didn't…"

She smiled sweetly.

He'd been had.

"We'll start with forms of address for elected
officials."

"You mean jerks in office?"

"Well, we've got our work cut out for us,
haven't we?"

He looked at the eaves of the barn, at the
cramped birds' nests and rotted wood.

"We certainly do," he agreed.

It was greeting elected officials during milking
the cows, how to address clergy while picking up

the eggs from the little hens, proper courtesies extended to foreign diplomats while stringing wire fencing around the coop and small talk with company presidents while pulling little slivers of wire fencing out from under Chessey's fingernails.

"I told you to put on the work gloves," Derek said, holding up the first-aid-kit tweezers to show off an inch-long thread of metal. "Now you've ruined your manicure."

She bit her lip but didn't cry. He had to admire her for that.

"Just remember that a cardinal is called 'Your Excellency' and an archbishop is referred to as 'Your Eminence.'"

"You already told me that."

Derek was frankly relieved when Pappy came out to the barn to announce lunch—he didn't think he could take much more of Chessey's help.

"When you are seated between the ambassador to the United Nations and the archbishop of New York, which person do you talk to first?"

"Whichever one of them is the most interesting."

"Derek!"

Pappy stared over a forkful of green beans.

"Chessey, give it up, I'm not going to dinner with an ambassador and an archbishop," Derek warned. "I'm staying here."

"I'm going to persuade you to come with me."

"How?"

The question hung provocatively unanswered. She stared at him, her mouth opening and closing. Suddenly, he knew what she was thinking. If he were quicker, he would have thought that way himself before she beat him to it.

"Not in that way," she said crisply.

"I didn't say a word."

"You didn't have to. You just had that look on your face."

"He's had that look on his face since he turned thirteen," Pappy observed. "That's when the girls started coming 'round here."

The telephone rang, and Derek got up to answer it. When he returned to the table seconds later, he announced he was going out to play some pool after supper.

"I'll go, too," Chessey said. She started to tell him that she had played pool with her uncle at his club in Washington, but Derek abruptly cut her off.

"You're not invited."

"I know."

"You're not welcome."

"I know."

"This isn't your kind of people."

"You don't know what kind of people are my kind of people."

"Chessey, didn't anybody ever tell you that it's impolite to invite yourself?"

"Yes, but I'm not letting you out of my sight. It's a—"

"I know. I know. A free country," Derek said sourly. "But you call everybody by their names. No eminences or excellencies or highnesses."

Pappy chewed his food thoughtfully and swallowed.

"Do you want me to tell you what I'd do if I was seated between Demi Moore and Julia Louis-Dreyfus?"

After lunch, the work level intensified. Chessey couldn't make herself heard over the tractor's engine, and besides, it took every ounce of her energy just to keep up with Derek. When the sun finally reached the western mountains, Derek announced that they had gotten a "fair amount" done for one day.

"We'll head out for pool as soon as supper's done," he said. "You might want to change. You look a little worse for wear."

An understatement.

The damage was severe—her nails were torn to the quick, dirty besides. Her nose and cheeks crimsoned by the sun. The T-shirt and jeans muddy beyond belief.

A shower would take care of a lot of this, Chessey thought. And then she noticed two little patches of pink fabric lying on Derek's bed.

"I put your suit in the wash," Pappy said, stepping into the bedroom behind her. He handed her a plush white towel, still warm from the dryer. And three gold buttons. "I think it shrunk a little bit. I'm sorry. I noticed from the buttons that came off in the dryer that it was by Chanel. Must've cost you a lot of money."

Actually, it had cost her cousin Merriweather a lot of money. And it was last year's money. Or maybe the year before that, because Chessey could hardly remember when the suit had been handed down to her.

"Mr. McKenna, I may have to borrow another pair of your jeans," she said, thankful she had washed her underwear in the sink and that she always carried an extra set for emergencies.

"To go play pool? You're out of your mind. Women dress up around here for a Saturday night. They work all day in a pair of overalls and when they wash the sweat and clay and grit off of themselves, they want some glamour."

"Well, I can't wear this," she said, fingering the shriveled crepe wool and silk blend. "I couldn't use this skirt for a leg warmer."

"Let me give some thought to this matter. Here, take this can of naval jelly when you get in the shower."

"Naval jelly?" Chessey looked doubtfully at the jar of blue-green grease.

"Yeah, works a lot better than soap. And you need it."

After Pappy left, she got to work in the shower. She had never felt so dirty going into a shower and never felt so clean coming out. She wrapped her towel around her and took another look at her suit.

She assumed the knock on the door was Pappy and was surprised when a hard, muscular arm shoved in a handful of black cloth. Derek lobbed her pumps, clean and polished, onto the floor.

"Try it on," he said from behind the door.

"It makes a nice T-shirt," Chessey said, pulling the Lycra over her head. She shoved her feet into her pumps. Without stockings, they looked a lot less ladylike, a lot more provocative. She finger combed her wet hair.

"It's not a T-shirt," Derek insisted. "I ran over to the neighbor's house to get it. She said it's a dress."

"She must be mistaken."

"It's a dress. I've seen her in it."

"I'll bet you have."

"Chessey!"

"It's too short. My grandmother would throw a fit if she could see me."

"Well, she can't see you."

"It barely covers my..."

He shoved open the door.

He blinked twice, as if adjusting to a brilliant

HOW TO PLAY

"PINBALL WIZ"

and be eligible to receive
THREE FREE GIFTS!

1. With a coin, carefully scratch the silver circles on the opposite page. Then, including the numbers on the front of this card, count up your total pinball score and check the claim chart to see what we have for you. **2 FREE** books and a **FREE** gift!

2. Send back this card and you'll receive brand-new Silhouette Romance® novels. These books have a cover price of $3.50 each in the U.S. and $3.99 each in Canada, but they are yours to keep absolutely **FREE**!

3. There's no catch. You're under no obligation to buy anything. We charge you nothing for your first shipment. And you don't have to make a minimum number of purchases — not even one!

4. The fact is, thousands of readers enjoy receiving books by mail from the Silhouette Reader Service®. They like the convenience of home delivery and they like getting the best new novels before they're available in stores...and they love our discount prices!

5. We hope that after receiving your free books you'll want to remain a subscriber. But the choice is yours — to continue or cancel, anytime at all! So why not take us up on our invitation, with no risk of any kind. You'll be glad you did!

FREE
MYSTERY GIFT!

We can't tell you what it is...but we're sure you'll like it! A free gift just for accepting our **NO-RISK** offer!

DETACH AND MAIL CARD TODAY!

CLAIM CHART

Score 50 or more	**WORTH 2 FREE BOOKS** PLUS A MYSTERY GIFT
Score 40 to 49	**WORTH 2 FREE BOOKS**
Score 30 to 39	**WORTH 1 FREE BOOK**
Score 29 or under	**TRY AGAIN**

YES! I have scratched off the silver circles.
Please send me all the gifts for which I qualify. I understand that I am under no obligation to purchase any books, as explained on the back of this card.

315 SDL CPPY   215 SDL CPPQ

Name: _____
(PLEASE PRINT)

Address: _____ Apt.#: _____

City: _____ State/Prov.: _____ Postal
Zip/ Code: _____

The Silhouette Reader Service® — Here's how it works:

Accepting your 2 free books and mystery gift places you under no obligation to buy anything. You may keep the books and gift and return the shipping statement marked "cancel." If you do not cancel, about a month later we'll send you 6 additional novels and bill you just $2.90 each in the U.S., or $3.25 each in Canada, plus 25¢ delivery per book and applicable taxes if any.* That's the complete price — and compared to the cover price of $3.50 in the U.S. and $3.99 in Canada — it's quite a bargain! You may cancel at any time, but if you choose to continue, every month we'll send you 6 more books, which you may either purchase at the discount price or return to us and cancel your subscription.

*Terms and prices subject to change without notice. Sales tax applicable in N.Y. Canadian residents will be charged applicable provincial taxes and GST.

light. Then he stared. So long and so intently that she felt naked. Even without the scanty Lycra that she would have to concede was intended by its manufacturer to be a dress.

"Whoa, darlin'," he said.

"You said you call all women darling," she said, squelching a smile.

Washington, D.C., was a city of stuffed shirts and not a lot of gentlemanly attentions—and even she wasn't all business all the time.

"I never meant it like I mean it now."

They met each other's eyes, a little like children having a stare-down, a lot like adults taking their time.

She looked away first.

"You think I'll look out of place?"

"No more so than any other beautiful woman."

She swallowed. He reached out, nearly touching the base of her throat where a blue vein pulsed beneath clear skin.

"If you're going to follow me around all night," he said, snatching his hand back, "you'd better come on. Let's eat."

"I'm famished. What's for dinner?"

"Fried frog legs."

Chessey stifled her nausea. *He's just trying to scare me off,* she told herself. *If I ask for something different, he'll happily drive me to E'town to get it...and leave me there.*

"Mmm. Frog legs sound wonderful," she said, delivering her words with a gracious smile. "All the best French restaurants serve it."

Derek McKenna was true to his word and his character. He called every woman in Jake's pool hall darlin' and every woman loved him for it, judging by the lipstick smudges on his cheeks. But he was equally regarded by the men, who reached out to touch his shoulder, some slipping a "glad you made it out" into the quiet spaces between raucous whoops and cheers.

"Washington, huh?" the bartender asked Chessey, putting a soda glass on top of a napkin in front of her. He followed her gaze to Derek, who had been borne by the crowd of well-wishers to give his greetings to the older folks who sat at the window booths. "You two fixin' to get married?"

"No," Chessey said.

"Then it's a wonder Pappy let you in the house. He's pretty conservative with Derek. Comes from the fact that Derek could turn a pack of otherwise respectable girls plum boy crazy with just a glance. They'd be calling at all hours, coming out to the farm, mooning after him in school, asking him to tutor them in subjects they could just as well have learned out of a book."

"A ladies' man."

"But in a nice way," the bartender said, wiping

down the counter. "Derek is always honorable with his women, and that's why men like him. He's a good one and we're glad he's home for good this time."

"He'll be leaving tomorrow night for New York."

The bartender did a double take.

"Does he know that?"

"He knows I want him to."

"Miss, let me give you a little piece of advice," the bartender said, threading his dish towel through his apron sash. "He's a strong-willed man. He does what he wants. If you don't have a good reason for him to want to go, he won't. And, exceptin' the Army, I don't think he's one for taking orders. 'Course, after what he's been through, he probably wouldn't be for taking orders in the Army, either."

She looked at Derek, deep in concentration as he chalked a pool cue. She had spent a whole day prepping him on what to do once he was in the public eye, but she had always assumed that some light bulb would pop off in his head and he'd just do his duty to his country. He looked pretty comfortable right where he was, in the center of a group of friends. How could she persuade him to trade that comfort for a thirty-day whirlwind tour of the USA?

"Thanks for the tip," she said, pulling a five-dollar bill from her briefcase and putting it on the counter.

"Thank you, miss."

She studied Derek for several minutes.

And then she made her move.

"Oh, Derek?"

He looked up from his pool cue as if he had been caught with his hand in the cookie jar.

"Yes, Chessey?"

"Would you teach me to play pool?"

"Why?"

"It looks interesting."

The crowd around the pool table looked at her. Chessey thought her dress might be riding up. Or perhaps she was overdressed. But while the men wore clean button-down shirts and blue jeans, the women were another matter. The same women who had no doubt spent their day pulling tractors, hoeing fields, milking cows, tending fences and chasing after children had worked a glamorous magic for night.

Chessey's dress wasn't their quibble. It was the pool playing. *This is going to be harder than I thought...*

"How would I have ever gotten the chance?" She sniffed daintily, as if the blue chalk was irritating her nose. "It's not the sort of game my family played."

"Then why do you want to know now?"

She tilted her head till her hair fell forward over one eye.

"As I just said, it looks interesting."

He narrowed his eyes.

"What are you doing, Chessey?"

"I just want to play pool."

He stared at her hard. His eyes narrow, a crinkle of sunburn at each eye. She kept her gaze steady. He handed her a cue stick.

"All right, here's the white ball, and I'm going to lay the red ball here. Directly in front of the pocket. Put her in."

Chessey leaned carefully onto the table, looking back once to make sure that her modesty was intact. She tugged at her hem and smiled at him with what she hoped was helpless charm.

Then she plugged the stick home. The red ball skipped onto the floor, and the white ball ended up in the pocket. A friend of Derek's picked up the red ball and put it on the felt.

"Great! Do I get a point for getting the white ball in?"

"No, Chessey, you actually lose a turn for doing that."

"That doesn't seem fair," she said. "You're just fooling me."

"That's the rules of the game."

"Explain the game to me, then."

For the next ten minutes, Derek explained pool.

So did three of his friends, an ex-girlfriend who was now a mother of three and clearly the best pool player in town, and even the bartender threw in some hints on the game.

"This is too overwhelming," Chessey said. She shook her head. "I can't do it very well. I could never, ever learn to play this game."

She wondered if a single tear would be effective or too much.

She decided too much.

After all, he was a smart man.

"You can learn," he encouraged her.

"No," she said, tossing her head mournfully. She handed him the cue stick. "Is this what you used to do before you went in the Army?"

He nodded.

"He was pretty darned good," one of his friends told Chessey. "The best."

"Did you bet money on it?"

"He never had to pay for his round with his own money," the friend boasted on Derek's behalf. "He would always use his winnings to pay."

"You're the kind of woman who disapproves of betting," Derek observed.

"Of course I do. My grandmother would disapprove if she even knew I was here. Oh, Derek, I just had the greatest idea."

"I don't ever like your ideas."

"You'll like this one."

He crossed his arms over his chest.

"Okay. Start talking."

"You don't want to go to New York. I want you to go to New York. We could argue about this forever."

"Or until tomorrow night," Derek said.

"How about if we settle it right now?"

The room fell quiet, so quiet that the clunk of ice rolling out of the ice maker sounded like a jackhammer.

"What have you got in mind?"

"One game," Chessey said, advancing on him. She put one hand on his chest, hoping that if he made her heart race she could do the same for him. Put him off balance. Make him falter. "One game. You win—I go back to Washington tomorrow. I win—you come with me to New York."

"Uh-uh."

"Come on, Derek, you can't be that scared of losing."

She was banking on the universal inclination of men to not want to lose face in front of their friends.

"Chessey, I'm not very good at pool," Derek said, taking her hand and putting it firmly on the cue stick. "I haven't played in a long time. Prison, you know."

"Oh, I know. But I've never played. It'd be an easy way to get rid of me. If you want to."

He stared at her long and hard. She willed herself to not blink.

"Next flight out of the E'town airfield is in four hours."

"You're on."

Chessey smiled approvingly.

"Do you want to go first or should I?"

"You go first," Derek said.

"Then let's—how do you say it?—rack 'em up," Chessey said, swiping a cue stick with chalk and eying the table.

She broke the triangle and put in the solid number four.

"Now that's gotta be beginner's luck," murmured the bartender.

Derek's mouth opened as if he was going to say something, and then he clamped it shut. He crossed his arms over his chest.

"Six ball in the corner pocket," Chessey said, nodding to the far end of the table.

And she did it.

"Derek, you might have finally met your match," a friend said.

Chapter Six

"I just have one piece of advice for you," Derek said, settling into the driver's seat of Pappy's truck. "Never try to con a con."

Chessey looked at him haughtily.

"Are you a con?"

"Had to learn to be. Only way my men survived. I got to be pretty good at lying, cheating, conning, stealing and just generally ignoring my conscience on all but one point—that my men were going to make it out of Baghdad or I would die trying."

Chessey shook her head.

"I nearly won."

"You did pretty good. Where'd you learn?"

She almost stuck with her story, but then decided there was no harm in him knowing the truth.

"My uncles belonged to the Cosmos Club in Washington. They have a private room where they play pool—my uncle Carson would take me up there when I was a little girl. And I played in the summers in the Hamptons when I visited relatives."

She didn't add that she would play her cousins for money so she'd have enough to pay her fair share of dinners and movies. She had, in her teens, regarded it as an issue of pride not to always be the guest. Pool was something she could do to even the scales. She had never met anyone she couldn't beat.

Until she met Derek.

"Tell me the truth, Lieutenant. You were never going to New York, were you?"

"No."

"And there's nothing I can do or say that will change your mind."

"No, Chessey, I can't do it," he said. "I've been away from home for so long I just wouldn't feel right leaving."

She nodded.

"I'll call the general tomorrow morning," he offered. "And your boss. What's his name?"

"Winston Fairchild III."

"Yeah, I'll call them all. I'll tell them you've done your best, and that you were almost but not quite persuasive enough."

His words were softly spoken, but they were firm and sure. It was time to give up.

"It's only two hours before the first morning flight. Why don't you drive me to the airfield?" she asked. "I've got my briefcase, and I'll give you money so you can buy the neighbor a new dress. Maybe even one with enough fabric to be decent."

"Chessey, I'm..." He started to say he was sorry, but if he did, he knew he would weaken his resolve. He had always been the kind of man women turned to, friends borrowed from, stray animals followed home.

He couldn't leave home again. Wouldn't let the night find him far from his own bed. Never let the nightmares find him far from home and vulnerable.

It was a weakness, he knew, but one he was powerless to overcome.

He turned the ignition and backed out of the gravel driveway.

A fine drizzle and the drag of windshield wipers were the mournful accompaniments to the forty-minute drive to the airfield. Derek knew he should feel relieved, even happy, that this Washington bureaucrat had finally given up. But instead, he felt like a villain. She scrunched onto her side of the seat and didn't look at him.

I'm sorry, I'm sorry, I'm sorry, he wanted to say.

But didn't.

The E'town airfield was bustling with activity. Rumsey Houchin ran a freight transport business on the side, and trucks were lining up by the hangar to be filled with produce brought in by prop plane.

Derek pulled his truck close to Rumsey's Jeep and reached for an umbrella behind the seat so she wouldn't get wet.

"Chessey, can't you understand?" he said guiltily. "I just can't go."

"Don't feel bad," she said, only making him feel worse because she was so understanding. "I actually think you deserve to do whatever you want after what you've been through. I was just pushing you because of my own selfishness."

"You mean—the government's selfishness."

"No, mine."

He narrowed his eyes.

"How so?"

"Look, I don't ordinarily unload my feelings," she said. "I consider it poor taste. And I'm usually a rather soft-spoken person."

"Then what changed? Because one word I'd never use to describe you is soft-spoken. You are the most argumentative female I've ever crossed paths with."

"I am not!"

He didn't say a word. He didn't have to.

Chessey stared at him, enduring her own silent horror. She had turned into someone who talked back. She had transformed into someone who argues at the slightest provocation. She had morphed into someone who jumps on a plane with a change of underwear, a toothbrush and a single-minded determination to change someone else's mind.

No one—least of all Chessey—would or could recognize her in her present state. And not just because she wore a dress made with little more fabric than is ordinarily used for cocktail napkins.

What had changed her?

Was it the determination to get a promotion, to have something more to her name than a studio apartment, a basement office and a collection of hand-me-down designer suits? To have a suitable man, a better reputation, a toehold on respectability?

Chessey realized the answer as soon as she opened her mouth to speak. And she just as quickly shut her mouth, pursing her lips tightly.

She had been transformed by a kiss.

The kiss had put her off balance, had turned her upside down. Sure, she'd been kissed before. A woman didn't get to be twenty-four without having kissed a few...frogs.

And this kiss shouldn't have been something special, since Derek had kissed her with the reprehensible goal of making everyone in that State

Department office think he was a jerk. When all he really was was a hero. A hero who wanted to go home.

She touched her fingers to her lips, wondering absently if she could wipe it away and go back to being the woman she had been just the day before.

"You were telling me about why you've been so selfish," Derek said gently.

She shook her head.

"Come on, Chessey, what's wrong? Why does it matter so much if I go with you?"

"It's because my life's a mess."

"Could be. A frequent occurrence. It doesn't have to be permanent."

"Oh, it is permanent. I'm a bona fide failure."

"Women as young as you don't get to call themselves failures," Derek said. "You haven't had enough life to fail. Occasional messes are another story."

"No, I've done it. I'm a failure. I've been given all the advantages and I haven't done what I could with them."

"Meaning your family has money and you haven't made more?"

"Quite the opposite. I'm from the poor section of the family."

"Millions instead of billions?"

"Worse than that."

"You got pretty fancy clothes."

"Hand-me-downs."

"You played pool in the Hamptons. And the Cosmos Club is a pretty fancy club."

"The uncles would divvy up responsibility for having me for summer vacation. The rest of the year I was sent to boarding school."

"That still doesn't sound like poverty."

"It was. My grandmother would say it started with my father. He went to Las Vegas when he was twenty-five. He was supposed to sleep with the show girls, not marry one. But he did marry Mom, even though he was warned that he'd be disinherited."

"Was he?"

"Oh, yes. Lawyers were put into action dissolving his trust and rewriting his parents' wills the minute Grandmother received the telegram from Nevada announcing that he had done it."

"So what did he do?"

"Unfortunately, being a Banks Bailey, he had never trained for a job. Couldn't drive a truck since having a chauffeur meant never needing to learn to drive. Couldn't work in a restaurant because he thought cooking was something you did with a hundred-dollar bill and the first name of a good maitre d'. Couldn't teach because he'd never learned anything worthwhile."

"How'd they survive?"

"They didn't. At first my mother still went on

stage, but when she got pregnant with me, she couldn't keep her figure—or her job. From there it was a slippery slope of poverty. They both died in an apartment fire when I was eight. They were smoking and drinking way into the night and... Well, my grandmother got custody of me and paid all my bills. Every September I was given a lecture by her on the importance of doing my best to marry young and well in order to pay her back.''

''Did you?'' Derek was startled. He glanced at her left hand.

''No, I didn't do that even after Grandmother paid for a coming-out party so that I could meet suitable men. So I was sent to college and everybody hoped I'd at least do something important in government. I don't have a trust fund like my cousins—and every man who knows the Banks Bailey name also knows that I'm the poor one. And that I might at any moment revert to my mother's Las Vegas show-girl ways.''

''Will you warn me if you do?''

''No,'' she said firmly. ''I'm not going to. I loved my mother, but I'm not like her. Some men have thought they could take advantage of me in a way they would never dare...''

''If it weren't for your mother.''

''Yes. But I don't ever...''

''Ever?''

''Ever.''

"Ever?"

"Never," she said. "And I'm only telling you this because, well, I'm never going to see you again and you don't know any of my friends…"

"It's not the kind of thing I'd talk about with your friends. Or your enemies. Or anyone," Derek said.

"Good."

"But, Chessey, twenty-odd years and…never?"

"Twenty-four years old and a virgin. I've never had sex."

"Made love."

"I think, given the men that I've met so far, that 'had sex' is what they'd call it."

He shook his head.

"Miss Banks Bailey, I hope you can accept my apology for my behavior yesterday morning," Derek said. "It was a pretty low-down way of making my point."

"Which was?"

"That I'm not the kind of man the government would want representing it."

"I think the throwing peanuts up in the air and catching them with your mouth should have been sufficient."

"I embarrassed you."

"You did."

He sighed and looked away.

"Funny thing is, in other circumstances, I might

have wanted that," she ventured. She looked at the raindrops crawling across the window. "Well, I mean, not wanted it, but at least would have enjoyed it. This is too embarrassing to talk about. I should go now."

She tugged at the door handle, but he reached out and grabbed her wrist.

"Chessey, you're a good woman," he said. "You're bright, you're pretty, you try your best and you're nice to me even when I don't have a right to it. You go back to Washington. You'll meet a man who'll deserve you. Maybe even that Fairchild guy. And you'll get married, have some kids, get a few promotions. You'll forget about this feeling you have inside you."

"Sure, Lieutenant."

"You don't believe me."

"No, I don't. I've tried to be respectable, responsible and a proper Banks Bailey, and it hasn't worked."

"You could always be a farmer."

His words were lightly delivered, as offhanded as any of his other jabs, parries or thrusts. But the catch in his voice was telling.

She could be a farmer. She could be his kind of woman.

They looked at each other, faces illuminated only by the glow of the hangar's interior track lights.

They simultaneously shook their heads.

Pappy was absolutely right.

Pigheaded.

"You know, I could kiss you goodbye," Derek offered, rolling down his window to a rush of cool night air. "And for just a moment, you could stop being a Banks Bailey. No one would ever have to know about your lapse."

She closed her eyes.

She couldn't. She wouldn't. Twenty-four years in training to be a lady, a Banks Bailey lady, had to count for something.

But this was Kentucky, far from home. With a man whom she was never going to see again. On a dark night where no one could see her.

And she was a woman. There was the pull of womanly fulfillment.

"Yes, kiss me," she said. "Kiss me. But no more than one kiss."

She came at him with absolutely no savoir faire, no elegance, no confidence. Trying to repeat—or maybe cancel out?—their first kiss, she flung her arms around his neck and planted her lips firmly on his.

"Whoa, darling, no," he said, pulling her hands from behind his head. "Kissing isn't a contest or an argument or a battle."

"Well, when you kissed me before—"

"When I kissed you before, I was out of my

mind. And I shouldn't have done it. That's not how I kiss."

"Oh."

Chessey wondered if this meant he wasn't a good—

"No, darling, I'm good at it," he said, as if reading her mind. "But we're going to get a little comfortable first. You sit like this."

With an effortlessness that made Chessey feel like a doll, he pulled her to him so that she was nearly on his lap, squeezed between his firm chest and the steering wheel. She tugged at her dress, which rode up high on her legs as they stretched out on the passenger side.

"No, don't worry about your dress," he said. "That thing isn't ever going to cover up as much of you as you want it to. But I promise I won't touch."

He jerked his head toward his left arm and firmly planted his elbow on the open window ledge.

"See? Just a kiss, Miss Banks Bailey, nothing more."

And nothing less.

His index finger under her chin guided her to him.

"Close your eyes, Chessey," he whispered. "You'll enjoy it better that way."

She squeezed her eyes shut just as his lips

touched hers. First a tender brush stroke of flesh against hers and then, as she softened, his lips prodded her mouth open.

There came the explosion of sensation, beginning in her mouth and traveling to the warmth of her belly. Every part of her body wanted to be taken by him, wanted to be touched, begged to be a part of his—

"Hey, you all!"

Chessey startled, bumped the truck's horn, yelped at its honk and then jerked into the passenger seat, yanking the Lycra that just wouldn't stretch any farther than mid-thigh.

Rumsey Houchin shoved his head into the window right up close to her face.

"Does this 'strictly professional' relationship need to buy a ticket?" he asked.

"Rumsey!" Derek complained.

"I'm just askin'! Cuz the pilot says he wants to make an early start of his day."

"I was just leaving," Chessey said, scrambling for her briefcase. Rumsey Houchin jumped as she swung the door open. "Here's two twenties. Keep the change. Goodbye, Lieutenant, have a nice life."

She strode to the runway with as much dignity as her tight dress and heels allowed.

"Evenin', miss," the pilot said, helping her into the prop plane. "Didja enjoy your stay?"

"It was just business," she said, wishing she didn't sound so snippy but powerless to stop herself.

She forced herself not to look back. Even when the plane rose toward the trees, banked left and passed right over the little red pickup truck and the man standing beside it, waving.

She got to her studio apartment at nine. The street sounds from her single window were louder and more contentious than she remembered. Her upstairs neighbors were playing rap music again. The flowers in her window box were limp and brown. She opened the refrigerator—it was empty and smelled like a dirty sock.

When had she thought this life was charming?

On her machine was a message from her cousin Merriweather asking if she could plan on staying late at dinner next weekend because the cook said she wouldn't work after seven and there were sure to be dishes and Merriweather's husband didn't like a messy kitchen left overnight and would Chessey mind cleaning up?

"Thanks, Chessey, you're such a dear," Merriweather chirped.

The next message was from Winston Fairchild III, complaining that a check of the New York hotel where McKenna had been booked had called to say that the lieutenant hadn't showed.

"Chessey, you can kiss this job goodbye if you can't produce," he said with unnatural coarseness. "In fact, I'll have my secretary type up your resignation."

Chessey dropped her briefcase on her desk and curled up on the couch. The flight to Louisville, the connection to D.C., the cab ride in from Dulles Airport—she was exhausted. And she also felt a grief she couldn't quite name. Ordinarily, when returning to Washington on a business trip, she would gawk out of her window seat at the monuments and capital buildings. This morning, she had simply closed her eyes.

Her couch wasn't comfortable. She switched a pillow around. Put it over her head to muffle the driving beat of the upstairs neighbor's music. Still not comfortable. Maybe she needed the little throw. But putting it over her legs didn't satisfy her. Then she sniffed. First at her shoulder and then, tugging at the front of the dress, at its bodice.

Derek McKenna.

The scent of him on the dress.

Mint and musk, citrus and bay leaf.

She tugged off the scanty black dress and pulled a nightie out of her closet. She stood over the kitchenette wastebasket for several minutes, trying to decide.

She took the dress to the couch, curled up with a pillow, the throw wrapped around her legs. And the dress, its scent a comfort and a despair, clutched in her hand. She remembered the whine of the cicadas, the scent of grass, the feel of his arms around her...

She was awakened abruptly by the phone. Ringing right next to her ear.

Don't answer it, she thought. *It's going to be Merriweather calling to find out if I can come early, too, to set the table and cook the meal.* The machine picked up the call.

"If you'd like to leave a message, do so after the beep."

She waited for Merriweather's cultured accent, but instead heard Winston.

She lay staring at the ceiling as he spoke, wondering if she should pick up and tell him that she'd sign any resignation he wrote for her if he'd just have it messengered to her apartment.

"Chessey, dear, sweet, wonderful Chessey!" Winston exclaimed, sounding not at all like an ex-boss. "I know you're in New York, and I'm sorry I can't get hold of you there. Listen, disregard the message I put on your machine last night. I was confused. My secretary must have screwed up. Or maybe my assistant. But in any case, I take full responsibility for their mistakes...."

Chessey grabbed the phone.

"Winston?"

"Chessey, you're home! What are you doing at home?"

"You've asked for my resignation," she said. "I don't work for you anymore and I don't have anyplace else to go."

"Oh, yes, you do! Get back to New York. You do work for me. And, by the way, I'm thrilled."

"Why?"

"He is remarkable! You have coached him so well! He's wowing those aeronautics suits so completely that they'll be begging us to let them sell us their planes for less money. Poised, confident, heroic—he even held out the chair for the governor's wife! I'm watching him on C*Span and I'm stunned. How did you manage this transformation in just two days?"

Chessey tried not to let her soaring heart get in the way of a quick analysis of the situation.

"I'm very good at what I do," she said. "And I wanted that promotion you promised."

"You sure are good! When you're done with this tour of duty, you can have any job you want. By the way, mark it in your calendar that we'll do lunch when you get back. Next stop is Baltimore, right?"

"After the cocktail party given by the mayor this evening at Gracie Mansion."

"Well, keep up the good work. Goodbye, Chessey. You're great."

"Thank you and goodbye, Winston."

"Remember—lunch when you get back to Washington."

"Sure, Winston."

And then, and only then, did her boss hang up.

Chessey stared around the room, which had just an hour before seemed the most depressing hole in the world. She flipped on the television to C*Span, a channel watched only by the most hardcore political junkies. It broadcasts live from the floor of Congress, but on slow days, showed meetings from around the country. It had been rumored to be as useful in curing colicky babies as vacuum cleaners, washing machines and other monotonous appliances.

"I stand before you now a proud American," Derek was saying, to a packed ballroom of gray-suited men and women. The applause was deafening. With perfect timing, he surveyed the crowd, waited for the hush, and then continued. "And I love New York!"

Chessey stared openmouthed. He wore a dress uniform. He read from notes she must have left behind at the farmhouse, but still managed to keep eye contact with his audience. He smiled the smile heroes bestow on their faithful, he spoke movingly about the House bill presently under consideration by congress, but carefully did not take a position as the President had not yet done so.

A standing ovation ensued. The governor's wife kissed him, leaving a fuchsia lipstick mark on his cheek. The Archbishop of New York clapped him on the back and several suits crowded in for a final handshake, and the chance to appear on the evening news with Derek McKenna.

Chessey flipped off the television, grabbed a navy blue, a gray and a black suit from her closet and shoved them into a garment bag. At her dresser, she tossed unopened packages of panty hose into her briefcase. Flying toward the front door, she yanked panties and bras from the shower rail in the bathroom. And she flung the gallon of milk that had matured past its sell-by date into the Dumpster on the sidewalk.

Within a half hour, she was on the corner of Arizona Avenue and MacArthur Boulevard. She caught a cab to the airport and was temporarily daunted by the long line at the ticket counter.

Then she smiled.

She marched up to the agent, who started to tell her that the line begins over there, ma'am.

Chessey held up her State Department ID.

"Oh, yes, I remember you from a couple of days ago," the ticket agent said. "How may I help you?"

"State Department, official business," Chessey replied crisply. "I must have a seat on the first available flight to New York."

"Right away, ma'am," the ticket agent said. She glanced at the man she had been helping. "Sir, would you step away from the counter? This woman is on official government business. I'll be with you shortly."

Chapter Seven

Your Excellence.

Your Eminence.

Your Excellence.

Your Eminence.

Hey, buddy.

Derek blinked twice at the robed man in front of him, conjuring up an image of Chessey, trying to remember what she had said. He could see the grass around them, feel the surgical tweezers in his hand. He had been pulling metal slivers from her fingers. She had told him the difference between the title one uses when meeting an archbishop and meeting a cardinal.

What did she say?

But Derek found himself awash in memories,

none of them helpful for the Gracie Mansion cocktail party in New York. He kept getting distracted by the memory of her delicate, soft hands. The pale fingernails. The smell of talc and roses. The way she bit into her soft, full, shell pink lips when she didn't want to cry out.

"Hi, there," Derek said, clasping the archbishop's hand. "It's an honor to meet you."

"I am the one who is honored."

The archbishop smiled broadly and selected a caviar-dotted toast point from the silver tray proffered by the waiter. The Gracie Mansion front room was crowded. The archbishop wisely popped the treat into his mouth before a jostling of guests behind him could send any of the precious black pearls flying.

The United Nations ambassador maneuvered into the space between the two men.

"Your Eminence," she said, nodding to the archbishop. "Lieutenant, I'm delighted to meet you. And I understand you'll be addressing a small group of my colleagues tomorrow morning in Baltimore."

"Oh, yes, the UNESCO gathering. I'm looking forward to it, Madame Ambassador," he said, a flicker of movement at the front door catching his eye.

"I wanted to talk to you about the importance

of stressing in your speech international cooperation on issues of..."

"Pardon me, Madame Ambassador, I must excuse myself," he said. He strode through the crowd, accepting handshakes and congratulations but keeping his target in sight. He shouldered through the security guards explaining to Chessey that since she didn't have an invitation she was welcome to take herself right back out at least as far as the hosta-lined sidewalk of the mayor's official residence.

"This is State Department business!" Chessey wailed. Her garment bag was digging into her shoulder, her briefcase bulged ominously, her suit was wrinkled, her hair had pulled out of its chignon. In general, Chessey was looking considerably more bedraggled than Derek would guess a Banks Bailey liked to appear in public.

"That ID card doesn't mean anything," one of the security guards said. "It just entitles you to a fifteen percent discount on lunch at the State Department cafeteria."

"Besides, it could be a fake," his colleague opined. "There's plenty of girls trying to get a chance to meet the lieutenant. He's a regular sex symbol."

"Well, I'm not one of those kind of women!" Chessey exclaimed indignantly. She spotted Derek and blessed him with an expression on her face that made it clear she considered him the cause of her troubles. Complete absence of gratitude. "Lieutenant, would you please make clear to these men that you are with me?"

"Guys, guys," Derek said. "You heard the lady."

He took her elbow.

"Can one of you store her garment bag?" he asked, as the security guards respectfully stepped back. "What'd you do, Chessey, come right from the airport?"

"As a matter of fact, yes," she said irritably.

"I would have thought you would have started with a 'Thank you, Derek,' under the circumstances."

He steered her through the crowd to an empty alcove. If he had to guess, she was long overdue on sleep, food, water and a long, hot bath. He supposed he should forgive her being a little frazzled.

"I'm sorry, Lieutenant."

"Derek. If I'm going to do this, you have to play by my rules. Rule number one is we use first names."

"Okay, Derek," she conceded, dropping into the plush cushions of a love seat. She seemed to suddenly become aware not merely of her responsibility to him but also her responsibility to anyone who might observe her. She pulled two bobby pins out of her hair and tried, without benefit of a mirror, to repair the damage. "I'm sorry, I should have started by telling you that I'm truly grateful that you've changed your mind. I can't tell you what this means to me. I can't begin to explain—"

"Rule number two is no getting emotional. This is business, just business. Nothing personal."

Something caught fire in her eyes. She crossed her arms over her chest and tapped her foot.

"Why don't you tell me rule number three while you're at it?"

His Chessey was back, and while he felt uncomfortable with simpering gratitude, he felt just as strongly that she could at least be a little more...deferential.

He had never met a woman quite like her and he would have thought, given his tours in the Army, that he had met all kinds.

"Rule number three," he said, sitting beside her and jabbing a finger in her face. "I give you thirty days of my life. Not a second longer. I noticed that the last thing on the schedule is the White House dinner on July Fourth. Right after the fireworks, stroke of midnight, I clear out. And I never want to see you Washington types again."

"That's fine."

"It'll be your responsibility to make sure that none of them—not the general, not the State Department wonks, not even the President—bothers me. I don't even want a Christmas card."

A sharp breath. He knew what she was thinking, and he felt like a heel. She was thinking about their last kiss and whether she meant anything to him. He should explain. He should soothe her feelings.

He should tell her that she wasn't the kind of woman who could have an affair and say goodbye on day thirty without a whisper of regret. And she certainly wasn't the kind of woman he could take home to live on a farm. And he wasn't the kind of man who could kiss a woman and not want more. A lot more.

It was better, far better, not to start.

He stopped himself from telling her that she could send him a Christmas card.

"Thirty days. No more. That's fine," she said at last, nodding vigorously.

"And one last rule," he said. "Number four—and it's the most important one. If you don't finagle a job with a corner office, five telephone lines and at least two secretaries, I'll consider this thirty days to have been a colossal waste of time."

Her head bobbed in what he figured must be agreement to his terms. He got up and tugged at the elbow of a passing suit.

"Could you snag me and my friend here a beer?" he asked the well-coiffed, dazzlingly toothsome man. "I can't seem to work up an enthusiasm for champagne. I'm just not that kind of guy."

"Sure, no problem," the gentleman said, relieving Derek of the champagne glass that had been shoved in his hand the moment he walked into the mayor's residence. "Would a domestic beer be okay?"

"The best," Derek said.

He sat down, relaxing for the first moment since he had gotten up this morning for the flight out of E'town. New York had been a dizzying whirl of handshakes, hearty greetings, kisses on his cheek, flowers from well-wishers that piled up in the back seat of the mayor's limousine until Derek demanded that the blooms be taken to a nearby hospital and distributed amongst patients who didn't have any in their rooms.

"Do you know who that man was?" Chessey asked.

"No."

"That was the governor of New York."

Derek rubbed his jaw.

"Somebody needs to tell that man to get his wife some lipstick that doesn't smear," he said. "But they're a nice couple, so I'm willing to grant them a few faults."

"UNESCO is the heart and soul of our people," Chessey said, kicking off her heels. She wiggled around to get comfortable on the couch in the sitting room of Derek's hotel suite. She wondered fleetingly if she could get herself a room or if she should call Merriweather to ask for her key to the pied-à-terre they kept in the Central Park West neighborhood. Chessey looked at the legal pad propped on her knees. First things first. They were scheduled for Baltimore tomorrow morning, and he needed a speech. "UNESCO is how we show the world we care. That's pretty good."

A second chance.

She had been given a second chance. She didn't know why he had changed his mind and she sensed he didn't want to be asked. It was going to be business, all business, between them. Rule number two. No asking or answering personal questions.

But there was disappointment even as she looked forward to the opportunities that had been presented.

Face it, Chessey, she thought, *you were more affected by that goodbye kiss than he was.* After all, he was a man who had clearly had success with women. Three women had asked Chessey for his hotel room number at the mayor's party, and Chessey figured more had worked up the courage to ask Derek themselves. Derek had laughed when she told him about the women in the limousine to the hotel.

"I finally get the freedom to take advantage of life and I'm stuck working for you, so I can't do anything about it," he had said.

Chessey opened her eyes. How had she got to

dreaming about his ocean blue eyes and the way his Adam's apple jogged when he laughed?

When I'm done with this month, I should go out with some of those men that Merriweather keeps trying to fix me up with, she thought. *I've got to get out more. Have more experiences. Well, just a few. Not too many.*

"Cleveland," she murmured sleepily, forgetting Baltimore entirely. "Cleveland is the bread basket of America."

"Chessey, are you already thinking about day after tomorrow?"

"Yes."

"Why don't I just tell them I love Cleveland?" Derek called from the bedroom. "It seemed to work in New York."

He emerged from the bedroom wearing comfortable jeans and a cashmere-soft cotton T-shirt.

"Or I could be like John F. Kennedy and say 'Ich bein a Clevelander.'"

She didn't respond.

"You know, Chessey, maybe I should add a last rule that you have to be nice to me. Laugh at my jokes. Agree with me every once in a while. Act as if you don't think I'm a complete idiot. Okay? That's going to be rule number five from now on. Repeat after me—I, Chessey Banks Bailey, am going to treat Derek McKenna nicely. Chessey, come on."

He looked at the couch.

"And no falling asleep while I'm talking," he said. "You've got to learn how to pretend you're interested in what I have to say."

He gently slid the reading glasses from her nose. Put them on the legal pad, which had dropped to the floor beside her. Then he covered her with the coverlet from the king-size bed in the bedroom.

"Good night, sweet protocol specialist," he said, and then he sat on the plumply cushioned armchair across from her.

It was better than trying to go to sleep.

Anything was better than trying to go to sleep.

And for the first time since he could remember, he slept and his dreams did not take him back to a prison half a world away.

"Mr. King."

"Call me Larry."

"All right, Larry, the people here in Los Angeles are wonderful."

"I feel particularly at home, here in Indianapolis."

"When I leave tomorrow, I really will be leaving my heart in San Francisco."

"And when somebody asks me, 'Do you know the way to San Jose?' I'm going to tell them that I do—and that I want to come back soon!"

"Hello, New Orleans!"

If it was June twenty-third, then this must be Des Moines, Chessey thought, glancing out the window of the jet as it taxied to a stop. She made another check mark on the schedule calendar. Tomorrow it was back to New York, and then to Indianapolis.

That's a lot of frequent flier miles, she mused.

"Hey, Derek, wake up," she said, nudging him. "We're here."

He groaned.

"St. Paul has made this Southern boy feel mighty welcome," he muttered.

"We're not in St. Paul anymore. This is Des Moines."

He struggled upright, glancing around the nearly empty first-class cabin.

"Iowa?"

"Des Moines—" she nodded "—and then tomorrow, we fly to New York."

"The mayor again?"

"The Council of Economic Advisers."

He threw up a hand. He seldom cared to know who he was addressing.

"Did you call your boss?" he asked, pointing to the sky phone attached to the top of the tray table.

"You're looking at the Protocol Secretary for the State Department," Chessey said, nodding proudly. "Winston's very pleased."

"Corner office?"

"Yup. Eighth floor."

"Telephone lines?"

"Only two, but I've been promised more."

His brows furrowed.

"Two is a lot," Chessey pointed out. "The vice president only has two."

"All right. Secretaries?"

"Two of those, plus an unpaid intern."

"Dang it, Chessey, you've done all right."

"Just following rule number four. You haven't wasted your time."

He hadn't wasted a moment in his quest to give Chessey a career boost. Under her direction, he had been charming but forceful at the Chamber of Commerce convention in Chicago, sweet in a nearly boyish way with Barbara Walters, courtly with the League of Women Voters and impeccably capable of using the right fork at private dinners given by socialites in New York, Los Angeles and Houston. Squeezed in between the newsworthy events were the coffees at city halls, cocktail parties at business clubs, receptions at universities and luncheons at Rotary Clubs.

He was a tireless advocate of selflessness, attention to duty and devotion to the country that had given him life. He tapped into something people desperately needed, because Chessey often had trouble extracting him from the hordes of autograph seekers, hand shakers and come-ons. Everyone wanted a piece of Derek McKenna, and he wanted to oblige. He had to rely on her to say no when the day got to be too much.

He also had the most annoying habit of emptying his pockets of the wadded-up scraps of paper with phone numbers that had been slipped to him by waitresses, socialites, matrons, flight attendants, hotel liaisons and models.

"So many women," he'd say with mischievous grin as she recoiled. He had assigned her the task of putting them in the shoe box he kept in his duffel after she complained that the line of his uniform was ruined by all the paper in his pockets. "But, oh, so little time."

The jet turned, approaching the gate. Chessey gathered her papers and shoved them into her briefcase. The flight attendant had unbuckled herself and had come over to Derek with a slip of paper with her phone number.

"Lieutenant, you give me a call if you're ever out this way again," she drawled.

Derek smiled, thanked her for her hospitality, but carefully made no promises. He put the piece of paper into the breast pocket of his dress blues.

"You could start your own telephone directory," Chessey whispered as soon as the flight attendant was out of earshot.

"Jealous, Chessey?"

"Of course not," Chessey said, feeling her face

turn crimson. "I'm just curious—do you call any of them?"

"No. All of them want Lieutenant Derek McKenna, hero. Not a one of them's interested in a farmer."

"Especially not one who charms a girl by telling her that cottonmouths, copperheads and water moccasins are going to come get her when she's sleeping."

He shrugged.

"Why don't you throw them out?" Chessey asked with more sharpness than she intended.

"Because it takes a lot of courage for a woman to approach a man, and throwing out a phone number seems downright mean."

"It seems downright arrogant to keep them."

"Don't stick your claws out too far, Chessey," he warned.

They let the other passengers go ahead of them. Some stopped to get Derek's autograph or say a quick word, but most had already talked to him at some point in the flight. He had taught a ten-year-old who had been a little skittish about flying how to throw peanuts in the air and catch them with his mouth. The two had performed for the ten-year-old's mother, who had kissed both Derek and her son.

Chessey reached over and rubbed the Cherries in the Snow stain off his cheek.

When the plane was empty, Derek and Chessey retrieved their bags from the overhead compartment. The flight attendant kissed Derek on the cheek, and he told her three times how he was grateful for how she made his flight more comfortable.

"What's the mayor's name?" he asked Chessey as they approached the gate.

"He is referred to as the Honorable—"

"No, Chessey, his first name."

"Bud."

"His first name is Bud?"

"Yeah, Bud. But you refer to him as the Honorable—"

Derek took a deep breath, shifted his garment bag to his left shoulder and entered the airport with his right hand extended. The stark camera light was nearly blinding.

"Hello, Bud! How you doin'?" he exclaimed, and as the local news outlets swarmed, he shook hands with the mayor of Des Moines as if they were best friends.

Which, judging by the mayor's ruddy-cheeked smile, they were.

Even if they had just met.

Chapter Eight

"Chessey, this simply won't do," the gravelly voice said without preamble.

"Grandmother," Chessey said, steadying the phone at her ear as she patted the nightstand looking for the lamp. Thursday. Must be New York. "Grandmother, so good to hear from you."

"You can't do this to yourself." Her grandmother's voice cracked—or maybe it was a bad connection. Still, her next words were sharp and clear. "And you cannot do this to your good name and to your family."

"Do what?"

"Strong condemnation must be expressed in strong language," her grandmother continued. "So Chessey, I must tell you that you are acting...like a tramp."

Chessey closed her eyes.

"A tramp?"

"Yes. I have it on good authority that you have been cavorting about the country with a man. Unchaperoned."

Cavorting. A man. Not just any man. Lieutenant Derek McKenna.

"Grandmother, it's business."

Well, except for two tiny kisses...

"Business? It cannot be a proper young lady's business to be a man's plaything."

"I'm not a plaything. I'm a protocol specialist."

"You are bringing scandal onto this family. We only just survived the shock of your father's wedding."

"That would have been twenty-six years ago."

"Still." She sniffed.

"Grandmother, this'll be over in just a few more weeks."

"The humiliation will last a lifetime. Chessey Banks Bailey, do I have to remind you of your origins? From both sides of the family?"

"No, Grandmother," Chessey said, defeated. "You don't have to remind me. But I'm not sleeping with him. His hotel room is two floors above mine. We've never shared a room."

Except the first morning in New York, when she had awoken in his suite. But he had been still sleeping in the armchair across from her couch when she had showered and dressed. Neither of them had gotten near a bed. Or each other.

"It's appearances that matter in this situation."

"Grandmother, it's my job to shepherd the lieutenant through a month of goodwill appearances. This isn't any different than what I do for ambassadors, diplomats and civil service employees every day."

"You don't do it all over the country. And you don't do it in hotels. And you don't do it with a man who looks like a movie star."

"This is my job!"

"You need to quit your job if they're going to use you as a...comfort woman. Get yourself back up here to the compound and we'll find you a suitable husband. It's something I should have put more effort into years ago. We won't have many men who'll take you—given your history. But if that doesn't work, you could always live with Merriweather and her husband. Their children could use some looking after. You could make yourself useful."

"Grandmother, I haven't done anything wrong."

"Chessey, think of everything you're sacrificing for this man. Including my respect."

And her grandmother hung up.

Chessey stared at the phone for several minutes, feeling as if she had chewed up five pieces of bubble gum and swallowed them all at once. Then she laid her head on her pillow and cried. She was still crying fifteen minutes later when Derek knocked on her door.

"Hey, I wanted to ask you about what you meant by this phrase you put in the speech for tomorrow."

She turned away from the door, went back to bed and pulled the covers over her head.

"Hey, this is serious," Derek said, standing at the end of the bed. "What happened?"

"You wouldn't understand."

"Try me."

She yanked back the covers. She knew her face was red and splotchy—she wasn't the kind of woman who became delicate and wan when crying. She knew her hair was a mess and her teeth needed brushing. She knew her Tweety-bird nightshirt looked ridiculous. But she didn't care.

"My grandmother called. She thinks I'm a..."

Her lip started quivering.

"Don't say it," Derek said. "I can guess. You want me to talk to her?"

"It'll just make it worse. She'll think you're covering up for me."

"Why does it matter so much what she thinks? I thought you said you hated it so much. The respectability, the rules, the hand-me-downs."

"It matters because...because...because I want them to respect me!" she wailed.

And in that moment, she was as exposed as a child, as vulnerable as the day she had been orphaned. The raw need on her face tore at his heart. He came to sit beside her.

"Aw, Chessey, you don't want their respect. You want their love. I've always been sure of Pappy's love, but you've never been sure of theirs."

She bit her fist, miserable as she conceded the truth.

"I'm so sorry," he said. "I'm the one who brought this down upon you."

"It's not your fault. No matter what I did, she would think the worst of me. She always has."

She turned away from him, her hair lying across the pillow like a golden ribbon, her shoulders quivering with grief.

"Chessey, darlin'," he said. He touched her face. She flinched. He backed off. And then she reached her hand out to him. He slipped off his shoes and gently, very gently, lay on the bed beside her.

She didn't protest when he put his arms around her, pulling him to her spoonwise, kissing an errant lock of hair as it brushed against his face. She stiffened only when he molded his body to hers.

"Chessey, you can beg all you want," he said

laconically. "But I'm keeping my clothes on and I'm just...here for you."

"I'm so tired," she said. "It was a long day and yesterday was a long day..."

"And the day before that was a long day."

"And I was just getting to sleep!"

"So go back to sleep."

"I'll never be able to."

"Okay, don't, then. You know, Chessey, I have trouble sleeping."

"You do not. I've watched you take naps in planes, trains, cars, buses, in chairs, couches, BarcaLoungers."

"Why do you think I need naps?"

She wiggled around so her nose was inches from his.

"Why do you have so much trouble?"

"It started when we first got captured. I just—" He jerked away from her and sat up. "Hey, I shouldn't be doing this. If your grandmother could see us, she'd have a fit."

She started to tell him it was okay, but she stopped herself.

"You're right. I don't think it's a wise idea."

"No, it isn't," he agreed. He stood and looked out the window at the glittering skyline. "Hey, I was going to sit up and do some reading. Mind if I do it here?"

He looked at the armchair on the other side of

the room. She looked, measured the distance with her eyes and nodded. She punched her pillow to get it just the right softness, pulled the blanket just so and settled into the part of the mattress that wasn't too soft or too hard.

"Oh, Derek?"

"Yes, Chessey?" He looked up from a guide to tourist attractions in New York, which he had picked up off the coffee table.

"If you start to fall asleep. I mean, just if you do, there's an extra blanket and a pillow in the closet."

"Thanks, Chessey."

She went to sleep easily, feeling protected by his watch over her. Still, she wondered at the demons he must fight with every day. And every night.

When the alarm clock went off at six-thirty, he was gone. But the blanket and pillow on the chair confirmed his presence. When they met in the lobby to catch the airport shuttle bus, he seemed unusually gruff. She didn't mention the previous night. He didn't, either.

During lunch at the Rotary Chapter of Indianapolis, a waitress serving the soup course slipped Derek a tightly folded piece of paper. Derek unfolded the note, read it, gave a lopsided grin to the messenger who was already spooning gazpacho into the mayor's soup bowl. The waitress seemed pleased by Derek's response—so pleased, in fact, that she walked away with her soup tureen, utterly forgetting to serve the chairwoman of the League of Women Voters.

Standing at the kitchen exit, Chessey observed this and caught a glimpse of the smuggled paper falling to the dais floor like a lonely snowflake. She grabbed the waitress as she shouldered past her to the kitchen.

"Hey, what was that you gave to Lieutenant McKenna?"

The waitress tugged out of Chessey's grip on her sleeve.

"Who are you?" she demanded sullenly.

"I'm from the State Department."

"Washington, huh? Well, my business with Derek is nothing to you," she said. She shoved the soup tureen at Chessey. "And you can serve the next course."

The waitress strode from the kitchen and swung open the door to the parking lot.

Chessey put the tureen on the nearest counter. Waiters and waitresses, cooks and busboys surged around her, marshaling the roasted chicken and sweet potato puree for the next course. She walked into the dining hall and made a beeline for the dais.

"Derek, here's your revised copy of the speech," she said, crouching at his side. The hand that wasn't extending a sheaf of papers to him was patting the floor, looking for the note. "Pardon me, Mayor."

"Chessey, I thought you already revised the speech," Derek said. "In fact, I think you've revised that thing a hundred times. What else can you do to it?"

Chessey's fingers snagged the folded paper.

"My mistake," she said, smiling as she yanked the alternate speech from his hand. "You just go with the one you've got."

She slipped away to the kitchen, careful of the waiters bringing out oversize platters of chicken. Then she unfolded the note, telling herself she was going to drop it right into Derek's shoe box at the first opportunity.

It was a crude hand-drawn street map with a red-ink path that led from the hotel to a location marked with a big fat X. At the bottom, a warning underlined three times.

Fourteen hundred hours! Sharp!

Chessey folded the note and put it in the pocket of her navy blue suit skirt. This didn't seem like a typical feminine invitation.

He had given her the slip a few times. Two hours in Oklahoma City utterly unaccounted for. Six hours in Cleveland with no explanation. Four hours in Milwaukee, culminating in a panic at the federal building because she wasn't used to his ways and thought he was going to pull a no-show. But he never no-showed. Derek always was where his official schedule required him to be—his shoes polished, his dress uniform pressed neatly, his smile ready for action.

She had always imagined someone blond and beautiful, confident and sexually knowing, who would answer his needs in a way that Chessey couldn't.

And she had always known that even if she failed to acknowledge his right to the unaccounted-for hours, he would have reminded her how much he valued his freedom if she had asked.

Still, she copied the map, walked to the dais one more time and didn't quibble when he told her that the speech really didn't need changing. When he was introduced to the room after dessert was served, he noticed the note from the waitress had fallen to the floor. He picked it up, put it into his inside suit jacket pocket and gave a warm and heartfelt greeting to the Rotarians of Indianapolis.

At one forty-five, many of the guests had returned to their offices. Still, some lingered, gathering at the dais to ask for an autograph, tell about their experiences with the military or just be near the stardust that was a hero. Derek was patient with every recently introduced friend—but he glanced up when Chessey walked out of the kitchen. He raised his eyebrows in a question.

"Ladies and gentleman, the lieutenant is going to have to say goodbye," Chessey said, smoothly sidling through the crowd. "He has a packed schedule and if he's going to make his next appearance..."

Her words lingered in the air, a reproach to those who might unfairly monopolize the lieutenant. The crowd dispersed with the faintly guilty air of kindergartners accused of not sharing.

Derek was already on his feet and halfway out of the room, but still he managed to convey regret about parting.

"I've truly enjoyed my time in Indiana," he said to the mayor. "You all are so hospitable."

"We've got some time before tonight's flight," Chessey said, following him. "Did you want to play pinball? The arcade is in the hotel basement."

During certain layovers, when the type line on books and magazines caused eyestrain and uncomfortable airport lounge chairs wouldn't allow for sleep, Derek had plugged quarters into pinball and video games. He had even taught Chessey some moves.

"No, that's all right about the arcade," he said, quickening his pace. "But if you need change, I've got some."

"No, I'm not in the mood for pinball. Where are you going?"

"I thought I'd take a nap. Need some shut-eye. Incredibly tired."

He rubbed his eyes for emphasis.

"The elevator to your room is that way."

He glanced across the plushly carpeted lobby to the elevator bank.

"I think I'll take a walk first," he said. "Don't you have a speech to write?"

"No. Tomorrow you're walking in the parade and having dinner at the White House. You don't have to say a word all day."

"Oh, yeah, well, why don't you call Washington and make sure my uniform—"

"Your dress uniform is ready."

"Call them and check the room at the—"

"The hotel has a queen-size bed with four extra pillows on it."

"Feather or allergy-free?"

"Feather."

He sighed.

"Good job, Chessey, you're so organized. Why don't you take some time off? You've been working too hard."

He handed the uniformed doorman a five-dollar bill and was given his duffel with a pleasant, "Hope you had a nice stay, Lieutenant."

"Thanks for packing up for me," Derek said.

"Derek, where are you going?"

"I'll meet you at the airport. Six o'clock flight, right?"

He stepped to the curb just as a taxi swung to a stop so precise that its back passenger door handle grazed Derek's outstretched fingers. The taxi melted into traffic, and Chessey internally argued the merits of following.

He was entitled to his privacy.

On the other hand, he was an ambassador of national goodwill and if he got into trouble, it would be her mess to solve.

Still, he wasn't her business so long as he made it to the parade and the President's dinner party tomorrow night.

But she had to make sure he got to that dinner party.

Derek had done everything he had been asked to do, and there was no indication that he wouldn't make the flight to Washington.

He had never kissed her again, never directed his natural, easy flirtatious charm toward her, never once touched her except as their fingers met as he took her bags when they got too heavy.

What was wrong with her? Why should she mind? He wasn't her type, he wasn't her kind, anything that could possibly happen between them would be short-term, and she wasn't that kind of woman anyway, wasn't like her mother at all.

So she shouldn't care.

But she did.

All this debate took place within a three-and-a-half-second hesitation. And then her hand flew up, she signaled the next cab and she said to its driver, "Follow that cab."

On every available inch of the picnic table were laid bowls and platters and pitchers. Heavy on potato salad, cole slaw, corn on the cob, hot dogs and hamburgers with charred grill stripes and lemonade with wheels of lemon floating on top. A foam cooler had stronger drinks. The children, and there were many, caught crawdaddies in the creek. The men dragged four more picnic tables from across the woods, and the women laid on white cotton tablecloths.

Derek had asked the driver to stop at a highway rest area so he could change into jeans, a comfortable shirt and running shoes. No man could run bases in spit-polished dress shoes.

He didn't know many of the gang at the forest preserve park. His host was a guy he had done basic training with, but it wasn't important who he knew and who he didn't. These were his kind of people. None of them knew the difference between an oyster fork and a dessert fork, but every one of them knew what a hero and a friend was.

Introductions were quick, amiable and generally one syllable apiece. Someone suggested they play ball, but several of the women overruled that, pointing out that the salads would spoil if not eaten soon. No one argued. Paper plates were handed out. The woman who had dressed as a waitress in the hotel ballroom wore a yellow sundress and she handed him a can of pop.

As Derek got his plate, he noticed out of the corner of his eye another taxi arriving at the preserve parking lot.

"Excuse me, guys," he said. And he added, "I'll just be a minute," because he knew he needed to prove that he wasn't a prima donna who was here just to shake hands and run. "Chessey, what are you doing here?"

She got out of the cab.

"I'm still in charge of handling you until Washington," she said crisply.

"Chessey, take the cab to the hotel. Read the tax code. Draw a diagram of a dinner party with the world's twelve most important people. Think of new things to regulate. I'll see you at the airport."

"No, I want to be here. I followed to see where you go," she said. "This is what you do when you disappear on me, isn't it?"

"We've only been in Indiana one day."

"No, but I mean there's places like this everywhere. People you get together with."

He nodded.

"How do they know how to get hold of you?"

"A buddy passes the word to the guys in the next town," Derek said. "This one's organized by a guy I barely know."

"But why?"

"It's my kind of people. Not yours. They're the kind of people that the guys in Washington sometimes forget."

She bristled and craned her head to look over his shoulder.

"Is there a…"

"A girlfriend?" he finished for her, smiling at the way her face crimsoned. "No."

"The waitress?"

"Wife of the guy organizing this. I'm waiting for the one I take home to Pappy, and there's not a lot of women standing in line to live on a farm."

"What about the women in the shoe box?"

The cabdriver leaned his pug face out of the window.

"Women in the shoe box?"

"It's just an expression," Derek said. "A shoe box is where a man keeps all the phone numbers that women give him."

"I could fit mine in a matchbox," the driver grumbled. "Now are you leaving or what?"

"No," said Chessey.

"Yes," Derek said.

"I want to stay," Chessey said. "Please, Derek,

it's the last time. And all I've got to go home to
is a hotel room.''

He shook his head. He couldn't believe how she
could turn on the lost-little-puppy-dog charm.

Or maybe she really did want to be with him.

"Fine, stay.''

The cabdriver peeled out of the lot.

Derek walked back to the picnic tables. He
turned around once, giving the fish-eye to Chessey's whisper-weight stockings, navy blue suit,
gray silk blouse and perfectly coifed hair.

"Don't you even own a pair of jeans?''

He didn't wait for a reply. He walked straight
to the buffet and put a big spoonful of potato salad
on his plate.

"Guys, this is Chessey,'' he said, moving on to
the cole slaw.

"Washington?'' one man asked.

"Yeah, but she's okay,'' Derek said, without
looking up from his plate.

His voice said, "Don't go there.''

Derek had been careful to push his fork around
at the Rotary lunch, so he had a good appetite for
the down-home food laid out. Somebody turned on
a boom box playing old Beach Boys tunes. Moth-
ers warned their children not to dig into cookies
unless they had eaten enough lunch. The picnic's
host handed Chessey a paper plate and told her to
start. Conversation was loud and punctuated with

laughter. Chessey praised the food, the punch, the beauty of the preserve, even the cheery pink napkins.

After lunch, a baseball game was organized with some of the women and most of the men. With some good-natured grumbling about men not being of much help, the picnic table was cleared and Tupperware containers returned to baskets and boxes.

Chessey helped with dishes, commented favorably on several babies and let one young girl try on her high heels.

As the sun started to slip in the sky, the baseball players realized they had forgotten to keep score and some of the men had developed a powerful thirst.

As the players abandoned the field, Chessey reminded Derek of their flight.

"Forty-five minutes," she warned.

"Ah, woman, it isn't time to go yet," he said loudly, and he accepted a beer from the cooler. "I wanna sit and visit a little."

He popped the tab.

"Tell us about it, Derek," one man said.

In an instant, the mood turned serious. The boom box was shut off, children shooed away under the care of their older brothers and sisters, and a semicircle of listeners waited on Derek. Chessey sat on the wet grass, deciding that Merriweather's suit could be sacrificed for this occasion.

He took a short pull on his beer.

"It was bad," he admitted. His audience nodded, understanding. "Any one of us on our own would have died. But we pulled together."

"Greg here is first cousins with a friend of one of your men," the host said.

"What's his name?"

"Bob," Greg said. "Private Bob Hosteler."

Derek nodded.

"Bob was a rock. He took care of some of the newly enlisted who couldn't cope with the tension and fear. How's he doing?"

"They got him in a hospital for exhaustion. He's not going to reenlist."

"That's too bad," Derek said. "He's a fine soldier. But I can't be too critical. I'm leaving the service to go back to my dad's farm."

Chessey recalled from the file that the private in question had been nursed back from dysentery by Derek. She noticed he didn't mention that.

"Why did they leave you out there?" one man asked. Others nodded. They knew what he meant.

"The suits in Washington didn't know where we were," Derek said.

"They left you for dead," a woman said.

"No, they didn't," Derek corrected gently. "They just didn't know. There wasn't any evidence we were alive. But we were never far from their thoughts. I'm willing to put my honor on the line for that truth. An officer never forgets his men. I didn't. And the guys in Washington didn't.''

''Even the generals?''

''Even the generals.''

The answer was what these folks had come to hear. Chessey had a feeling it was something that Derek had repeated, on his own, a dozen times in the past month.

''Chessey here works in the State Department, and they were always on the case. Right, Chessey?''

Chessey nodded, although she guessed that some of the picnickers sensed she wasn't so sure.

''The real point is that the men and women who go into the armed forces always take care of their own. I wouldn't have left that Baghdad prison if I had to leave one of my men behind. And none of you would have done any different. And the only difference between us and the generals is that they've done it a little longer than we have.''

He put down his plate and looked over to where the children were playing.

''This is worth it,'' he said. ''To come home to this makes it all worthwhile.''

''Welcome back,'' his host said and clapped him on the back.

The welcome backs echoed through the field.

And then someone volunteered to drive him and Chessey to the airport.

"I can't believe this is where you've been going," Chessey said, as the Ford Pinto merged with traffic. She sat in the back seat and talked quietly over his shoulder.

"Yeah, did you think I was out meeting up with a different woman in every city?"

She nodded.

"Oh, Chessey, I'm looking for something different," he said, sighing. "I'm looking for a woman who's simple. And who wants what I want. A family. A home. Some peace of mind."

"Here you are, guys," their driver said. "Good luck to you, Derek. Nice meetin' you, Chessey."

Derek went to the trunk, gave his host a hearty hug and picked up his duffel in one hand and her garment bag in the other.

"Oh, Chessey?"

"Yes?"

"She also has to be able to turn a tractor on a dime."

Chapter Nine

Mrs. Merriweather Banks Bailey Randolph met her cousin in the White House Vermeil Room, a sitting room reserved for women freshening up before joining the men in the Entrance Hall.

Chessey sat under the portrait of First Lady Jacqueline Kennedy, and Merriweather allowed herself only a moment of critical regard for the gold dress Jackie had chosen for the painting.

She could have done with something with a little waist, Merriweather thought, adding aloud, "Chessey, you look wonderful, darling. How are you?"

"Merriweather," Chessey said. "I'm so glad to see you."

Merriweather accepted a hug from her cousin and then stepped back, eying Chessey's dove gray jersey knit gown as she patted her hair for rebellious wisps. Had to be Marc Jacobs—this year's Marc Jacobs—and only a body like Chessey's could carry it.

Merriweather's flounces and ruffles and freshwater pearl buttons suddenly felt oppressive and outré to her.

"Did Cousin Margaret give you that dress?"

"No," Chessey said, smoothing the knit fabric over her slim stomach.

"But I didn't give it to you. It must have been Aunt Celeste's daughter Martina. She's always been a bit daring."

"No, Merriweather, I bought it myself."

"Yourself?"

"I splurged."

"You went to Marc Jacobs's design studio in New York? When did you ever find the time for the fittings? And besides," Merriweather added, "he's rumored to not be taking any new clients."

"I bought it at a department store."

"Off of a hanger?"

"Yes."

"It is a Jacobs, isn't it?"

"I wouldn't know."

"Turn around, let me see that."

Chessey turned around, and Merriweather pulled at the back tag.

Yup—an honest-to-goodness Jacobs.

Merriweather's perfectly glossed lips opened and shut.

"My little cousin," she said in her perfectly enunciated Philadelphia accent. "You always do have the strangest way of going about things. Bought a gown in a department store. My, my, but I forget that you are a busy professional. Congratulations on your promotion. I'm quite impressed."

"Thank you, Merriweather."

"And Grandmother says to tell you she's very proud." Merriweather's voice dropped to a whisper. "At the Rensselaers' summer party, she couldn't stop bragging about you. It was downright embarrassing."

"Really?" Chessey said, scarcely believing her cousin. "But I thought she was so upset."

"She was. Until she got a call from the President. He asked her—get this—asked her for her permission to send you around the country with the lieutenant. And then apologized—can you believe it!—for not having talked to her earlier, before you went off. Imagine—the leader of the free world groveling before Grandmother."

"What did she say?"

"To hear her tell it, she gave him a little dressing down for not having sent a chaperone with you, but pretty much forgave him. The President is quite charming, you know."

"I wonder why he called—"

"Your boss. Winston. That's the gossip, at any rate. He's watching out for you. In fact, I've sort of wondered if there's anything between the two of you. Didn't you have a crush on him?"

"I did. I don't think I still do. But then again, he's never said much to me."

"Well, he called me and asked if he could get himself invited to our summer party."

"Why would he do that?"

"So he could see you! Jeez, you are the most innocent little schoolgirl sometimes. Here's the details. Stephen and I are having our little summer get-together next weekend. We're putting a tent out in the back gardens for a picnic. Just two hundred guests. Plus Winston. It's going to be so precious. Say you'll come."

"And you want me to come early and dig the posts for the tent?"

"Oh, heavens, no! You're my cousin. You come at four o'clock for cocktails like all the other guests," she said, slipping her arm through Chessey's. Merriweather had a stab of conscience, wondering if she had ever treated Chessey as less than an honored relation, but she attributed the feeling to indigestion and popped a Tums from her evening minaudière. "But make sure you bring that dashing lieutenant I've been hearing about."

"Merriweather, he might not be available,"

Chessey warned. "He's been rather stubborn about going back to Kentucky."

"Well, he can go back there after next week," Merriweather conceded. "By the way, is this your first White House dinner? You look quite nervous. I've been here oodles. It's because Stephen is quite generous with his money—I mean advice—with many members of Congress."

When the President and First Lady came down the Grand Staircase with the Prime Minister of Paraguay, the President reached first to shake hands with Derek, who had been asked to stand at the end of the maroon carpet while most guests were cordoned off several yards away. The President presented Derek to the Prime Minister and his wife. Media were allowed a few pictures, some video feed of Derek engaging in small talk with the President and the Prime Minister, and then the Marines assigned to the White House hustled the reporters and cameramen out the door.

"Now we can relax," quipped the President. The room broke up in obliging laughter.

Standing with her back to the Entrance Hall wall, Chessey watched Derek with pride. No one would know that Washington was not his native soil—or that he had endured a four-hour-long parade in a typically muggy Washington summer afternoon.

He shook hands with amiable ease with diplomats, Cabinet members and senators when the cordon was taken down. He located and introduced himself to the wife of the Secretary of Defense he had been assigned to escort to the table in the East Room.

"You've done a good job with him," a voice at her shoulder said. She turned to face a blazing chest full of medals.

"Why, General, thank you," she said to the head of the Joint Chiefs of Staff.

"He's got natural charm and grace, a strong, courageous man," the general said. "And you've given him polish. All these traits would point to a stellar career."

"Unfortunately, he's going home to Kentucky to be a farmer," Chessey said, aware of the sadness in her voice.

"Still, the country's gotten a lot out of the man. I suppose he has a right to a new life. Speaking of new lives, congratulations on your promotion."

"Thank you."

"Just remember that if you aren't ever satisfied in the State Department, you've got a spot on my staff. A strong woman like you has a lot to offer her country. I predict big things for you, Chessey. Remember I said that when you're picked for a Cabinet post."

"I'll remember."

"Now, I have to find the wife of the Speaker of the House," he said, glancing at his watch. "It's because of you protocol types that a man can't simply have dinner with his wife. He's got to escort someone else to the table while his wife carries on with some other man."

"General, it's because you're the fifth-ranking man at the dinner and the speaker's wife is the—"

"Spare me," the general groaned good-naturedly.

Chessey was escorted into the East Room by a formally dressed Marine, one of many provided to single women of indeterminate rank. She couldn't help but be awed by the grandeur of a state dinner with all the most powerful men and women of Washington. The cut-glass chandeliers sparkled like a spray of diamonds, and the gold-and-white theme of the room set off the stark black tuxedos, medal-bedecked uniforms and evening gowns of the guests.

The meal was a typical seven courses, the conversation halting, although Chessey used her knowledge of the Spanish and Portuguese languages to build conversational bridges between the others at her table. She translated the President's toasts to the Paraguayan members of her table and translated the Prime Minister's toasts to the Americans.

"Are you related to the Banks Bailey family?"
one of the men asked. "You know, the ones that
came over on the *Mayflower*."

"Yes," Chessey said. It was a question she
heard often.

"Oh, but that's not the most interesting thing
about Chessey," the woman seated to his right
said. "She's the protocol secretary for the State
Department."

"Oh, really?"

Chessey felt her normally excellent posture become even more refined. She actually started to
enjoy herself.

Plates of tiny champagne grapes and wedges of
brie were placed next to full coffee cups as the
meal drew to a close. Derek walked over to her
table and asked her to follow him to the balcony.
The Chessey of last month would have told him
that nobody leaves the room before the President
on any state occasion. The new Chessey accepted
that he would do what he willed.

Besides, she missed him.

The day before, when they had arrived at Dulles,
he had been whisked away from her by Pentagon
officials. He wasn't her responsibility anymore.
She should be happy about that, but she couldn't
shake the wistful feeling of regret.

On the empty balcony overlooking the Presidents' Arbor, he popped open a bottle of champagne and poured two drinks.

"Where did you get this?"

"I have a friend in the kitchen," he said.

"You have friends everywhere."

"I'm lucky that way."

He tapped his glass against hers.

"To going home," he said.

"To going home."

"Oh, come on, Chessey, you look entirely too sad. You're getting everything you wanted. A new job, respect from your peers, White House dinners—I was introduced to your cousin Merriweather and her husband, and I'll bet that dress you're wearing is no hand-me-down from her."

"True."

"And I'm getting what I want. A shack in the mountains, crops in the valley, a couple of cows, the right to eat ice cream straight out of the container."

"True."

"Why do you look so unhappy?"

"I'm not," she protested.

"Did that Winston guy try to cheat you out of a raise?"

"Not at all. He's actually being rather nice to me. He got the President to call up my grandmother and smooth things over."

"Really?" Derek said, looking at her funny.

"Yes, he did. He's actually a very nice person."

"How very interesting."

He touched her glass with his once more.

"We've done all right. What a difference thirty days makes."

"I'm very grateful to you."

She dutifully sipped.

"Your cousin's husband tried to interest me in running for Congress."

"Stephen did?"

"Yes. He said I'd just have to snap my fingers to win the election—returning war hero, all that. If I'm a representative from Kentucky, he says I'd live in Washington three-quarters of the time. But I figure the one-quarter of the time I got to spend in Kentucky, I'd be chasing votes."

Chessey glanced up sharply.

"But you'd be helping your country. Maybe put some good back into politics."

"No, Chessey, I can't. You can never change Washington. Washington changes you."

In the western sky, the first fireworks exploded, illuminating the starkly simple Washington Monument. Chessey glanced at her watch. Nearly midnight. She felt a sudden urgency.

"Derek, I wish...." And then she could not speak.

"I know. I wish the same thing," he said kindly.

"But it can't be, Chessey. You know it can't be. Aw, don't cry, darlin'."

"I'm not crying."

He knelt in front of her, touching the damp of her cheek with the backs of his fingers.

"Chessey, I always told you I couldn't stay."

"I know." She gulped. "You never lied to me about that. But do you ever wish things were different?"

"Every day. But I know who I am and I need to be who I am. A farmer. That's who I am. I can't be a hero. I can't be a soldier. I can't be a politician. I can't be a player in Washington. I have to be a farmer. And I can only have one kind of woman—a farmer's wife. Chessey, you aren't a farmer's wife."

She nearly blurted out that she could learn but realized the utter falsity of the statement. However lovingly intended.

She was a city girl, a socialite who still had to prove her worth to her family.

She smiled bravely.

"Chessey, I have to go home. I have to be able to close my eyes at night and not be thinking, always thinking of...of what I saw, what I went through, the people I was responsible for. The ones whose lives depended on me. I got tired, very tired and very, very old in a way a man my age doesn't have a right to. I have to be able to rest and think about something other than conniving to make sure a prison guard doesn't beat one of my men until he can't stand up. I've got to be able to focus on something other than survival. I have to live in peace for a while. I can only do that at home. That's what home really means."

She reached out to touch his cheek.

"I might never really have had a home, but I do understand," she said. "And I know it took a lot out of you to give up this month for me. Thank you, Derek."

"Rule number two violation," he said sternly.

"Sorry."

They watched the fireworks for a few moments. Sounding like a distant firefight. He flinched, then held steady. She reached out and held his hand.

"Are you happy, Chessey?"

"I'm happy," she said, and she responded to his scrutiny. "I've got a great job, my grandmother thinks I'm okay, and I'm going to do what I wanted to do when I got out of college."

"And what's that?"

"Make a difference in the world."

He sighed. He had given up that dream for himself a long time ago, deciding that a man could only change his own corner of the world, and then only a little bit at a time.

But the world needed starry-eyed idealists, and her blue eyes made the night's stars seem drab.

"Good luck to you, then," he said.

And she knew she had to let him go. Her fingers slipped from his, and she stepped away, trailing her hand along the balcony rail.

The bells of St. Johns Cathedral began their toll.

"My long service to my country is over," Derek said, looking across the glittering night sky. "And now..."

A shiver coursed through Chessey as he put down his champagne and pulled her into his arms.

"I've wanted to do this all month," he said. "I've always wanted to do it the right way."

He kissed her. He possessed her mouth first with tenderness and then with deepening passion. His tongue entered her mouth and sought out every secret sensation, taking his own sweet time. The kiss deepened but then, of course, it had to end.

Reluctantly, he let go of her.

She clung to his shoulders, wanting with all of her soul for him to keep her in his arms even while knowing that he could only be the man he was meant to be if she let go.

"You deserve this," he said. "You certainly put up with a lot from me."

"You put up with a lot from me," Chessey said, working to steady her voice.

"Goodbye, Chessey. Look me up sometime when you want to kick back and relax in a down-home way."

"Will do," she said. So lightly. So offhandedly. One would think she was pleased to bring the month to a close.

He tugged at his tie as he left her, dazed and somewhat unsteady. He strode through the balcony doors just as a group of diners came out to watch the fireworks. Muttering excuse me to their enthusiastic greetings, he disappeared into the East Room.

Too quickly the month had gone by. She hadn't had a chance to tell him....

"No, Derek, no!"

She shouldered her way through the crowd coming out to observe the fireworks. She ran down the red-carpeted Entrance Hall, ignoring the formally dressed Marine who called out, "Ma'am, may I help you?" She quickened her pace, pulling the hem of her gown up nearly to her knees.

She reached the portico entrance just as a plain D.C. taxi pulled away. Just as Winston Fairchild III walked up with the Secretary of State.

"Chessey," he said, kissing the air at her cheek. "The secretary wanted to congratulate you on your new promotion."

Chessey absently accepted a handshake from the secretary. But as she moved off to follow Derek, Winston's voice stopped her.

"I called in for messages this afternoon," he said. "And got one to pass along to you from Derek's father—called himself Pappy. Said he was going to hold you to your promise. Any idea what he's talking about?''

She thought of the man waiting for his son. He had waited so long.

"Yes, if he calls again, you can tell him I haven't let him down.''

She had everything she had ever wanted. Dawn-to-dusk meetings that accomplished...a lot. Policy memos that would be read by the diplomats, Cabinet members and even the President. Planning conferences for diplomatic relationships that could result in real changes in international relations.

Although she was working fourteen-hour days, she wasn't too busy to notice the changes in her family. She had the respect of her cousins, who regarded her as an asset at their parties instead of a duty. Her uncles asked her advice in dealing with overseas businesses. Even her grandmother had softened her normally disapproving stance, going so far as to tell her that she was "quite proud" of her.

"Now if you'd just settle down with that nice young man from the State Department," she had told Chessey.

She was referring, of course, to Winston. He often brought Chinese food to her office when they were working late. Although he never discussed anything personal or made any attempt to kiss her, Chessey knew it was just a matter of time. The two of them had all the makings of a young Washington power couple.

While a month before, such a prospect would have thrilled, now Chessey regarded it more reservedly.

One late evening in August, Winston walked into her office and dropped a grocery bag full of envelopes on her desk.

"These are for you," he said. "Mail room's been collecting them."

Puzzled, she reached in and looked at the address.

"It's for Derek," she said.

"They're all sent in care of you," Winston said. "State Department won't give out his address. Open it."

"I can't. It's his mail."

"Are you going to send it to him?"

She remembered what he had said about not getting Christmas cards or any other correspondence.

"No," she admitted. She slid open the envelope, and took out a delicate slip of paper. "Dear Lieutenant, you may not remember me but we met in Albany, New York. I told you about my son who was sick with cancer. Cancer had put an end to his dreams of joining the Army. You agreed to meet him and you drove him out to the Army base to meet your friends and tour the base.''

Chessey remembered pacing the tarmac at the Albany airport. He had kept her waiting three hours.

"Keep reading," Winston urged. "This is interesting, in a mundane kind of way."

"My son Joey died last week, but I want you to know that that afternoon when you let him be part of your life was the happiest day of his."

Chessey swallowed and put the letter down.

"Wow," Winston murmured.

"I didn't know he did that," she said.

"I have a feeling if you open up all those letters, you're going to find more surprises like that."

"It won't just be shoe box ladies," Chessey agreed.

"Shoe box ladies?"

"It's just an expression."

Winston nodded.

"Chessey, have you ever wondered why I'm such a jerk?"

"You're not a jerk."

"Yes, I am. I'm making a difference every day in the lives of millions of people. I push through a policy position and a country gets aid money from the U.S. The next day, I might put together a delegation to give food to a starving refugee camp. But I never do anything good for the people around me. I wouldn't help my neighbor unless he was in another country. I don't think kind thoughts about a person unless they're a minimum of a thousand miles away. I'm rude to my dry cleaner, appallingly haughty to my doorman, and I never give my mailman a little something extra for Christmas.''

"And you're saying Derek's any nicer?"

"There's something to be said for being the kind of man who changes the world around him, not just the world he reads about or sees on television. Something about a man who helps the people that fate has put down directly in his path.''

"But you do do nice things for the people around you!''

"Name one.''

"Me. You called the President and told him to talk to my grandmother when she thought I was 'cavorting.'''

Winston shoved his glasses up the bridge of his nose.

"Chessey, the only reason I did that is because Derek McKenna told me if I didn't, he'd fly down to Washington and flatten my face.''

Chessey gasped.

"You know, for a Banks Bailey, you're awfully stupid. That man loves you, Chessey. He might not agree with you, might not do what you tell him to do, might act like an overaged boy one minute and a hellion the next. But he loves you, Chessey. And that's got to count for something in this world."

"Too pigheaded," Pappy said, pulling on his bifocals to read the menu at the recently reopened Brownsville Café. "Both of you are too pigheaded to admit you're in love."

Derek shook his head.

"It's not love. It was just an infatuation. I hadn't had a woman in a long time."

"Then how come you're not dating here? The phone's gonna tear right from the kitchen wall if it don't stop ringing. You got women from five surrounding counties chasing after you."

"I'm not interested."

"Harrumph."

Derek grimaced. He didn't want to discuss such a weakness with his father, but he missed Chessey. Missed her so terribly that sometimes he felt as if he had to handcuff himself to the house so he wouldn't fly to Washington and demand that she marry him.

He could have stayed in the Army—the head of the Joint Chiefs of Staff had told him that a Pentagon office was his for the taking.

He wrinkled his nose.

Or he could have gone to Washington—his name had come up when a television station in

Bowling Green had done an opinion poll on possible candidates for state representative.

Ugh—politics.

He could ask her to come to Kentucky, but the idea of Chessey mussing her hair or breaking a nail while working the farm was absurd.

He shook his head.

Impossible.

They were from two different worlds, had different ideas about how life should be. He glanced at his plate and muttered to himself that he needed to forget her.

His eyebrows tugged together.

"Pappy, what is this?" he asked, picking up his plate. It was ivory china, with an elaborate crest at its center and a brilliant silver edge. "I remember they had plain white plates."

"I suppose they did," Pappy said. "I'll have a hamburger with pommes frites."

"Pommes frites?" Derek asked. "What's that?"

"French fries," Pappy said. He glanced at the waitress. "Jeez, Derek, someone would think you'd been raised in a barn."

"I was," Derek pointed out. After all, when the farm hadn't been making any money and the roof on the house had been leaking like a sieve... Derek glanced again at the table. He picked up a small fork. "What's this?"

"That there is your fish fork," the waitress said.

"And here's your salad fork and your dinner fork. Up there over your plate is your dessert fork and over here is your soup spoon, teaspoon…"

Derek stood up, his chair legs scraping the pale wood floor. Several diners looked at him with mute disapproval. He looked around. Something about the people he had known all his life was different.

Missy Severns, the liquor store owner, was eating fried chicken—with a knife and fork!

Ned Senko and John Scherer, who jointly owned a tobacco farm up in the hills, were drinking coffee out of absurdly small china cups, their beefy little fingers extended.

Over by the window, the Houchin twins, known for being the biggest hell-raisers of the fifth grade, sat with their napkins carefully folded over their knees.

Linen napkins.

"And your knives," the waitress said uncertainly. "I didn't explain your knives."

"I don't need my knives explained."

"Derek, we all love having a little more civilized behavior," the waitress said. "And she brings it out in us."

Derek shoved past her to the swinging kitchen door. Chessey, wearing a white apron monogrammed with her initials, stood carving roses from tomatoes.

"When did you get here?" he demanded.

"Just a couple of weeks ago," she said. "I called Winona, and she told me about this place. Winston loaned me the money to buy it."

"Why'd he do that?"

"Because he said just once in his life he wanted to do something nice for someone."

"Why the hell didn't you tell me you were coming? I've wasted a few weeks of my life. Our life."

"I wasn't sure how'd you react. It's a lot of pressure to have a woman move to your hometown."

"Pressure?"

"The kind that keeps you up nights."

He closed his eyes.

"Chessey, I need you," he said. "I hate to admit it, hate giving in to it, but I need you."

"So it's okay? My being here."

"Did you at least give up your apartment and your job?"

She nodded.

"If it doesn't work out..." Her words lingered, her lips trembling.

"Stop your doubting. You know the kind of man I am. Simple as all get out. If I tell you I want you to stay, I mean it."

"I hope you're right. Because my cousins think I've lost my mind. My grandmother said she always knew that I'd turn out bad."

"You don't care."

"I don't?"

"You don't. At least, not as much as you would have ever thought. Because I love you," he said. And he kissed her long and deep. "Because you're a woman who needs love and needs to love. Love means more to you than starched-shirt respect. Your love is here, Chessey. And your home is right here."

He put her hand to rest on his chest. She felt his muscles throb against her fingers, his heartbeat matching hers.

"And besides," Derek said, "my pappy told me never to bring a woman home unless I intend to marry her, and I take the commandment to honor your parents very seriously. Chessey, will you marry me?"

"Do you think Pappy will approve?" Chessey asked. "After all, we're both pretty pigheaded."

"We'll just provide him with lots of entertainment when we fight," Derek said.

"We will not. He doesn't like it when we argue."

"He does, too. He thinks we're..." Derek stopped suddenly, realizing they were having the first fight of their engagement. "Chessey, I love you."

"I love you, too."

"And we can make it forever. That's what our marriage will be."

"Yes, it will," she said, feeling the power and simplicity of her words.

The kitchen door swung open, and Pappy strode in, regarded the couple embracing. He crossed his arms over his chest.

"If it wouldn't be too much trouble for you lovebirds, could I have my lunch?"

Derek grabbed a bag of chips from the counter, tossed it to his father and slammed the door behind him.

"Pappy doesn't have a sense of romance," he complained good-naturedly.

Chessey arched her brow. "And you're the romantic of the family?"

"Sure," he said. He kissed her lightly on the lips. "It's going to be love poems every day."

Chessey squeezed out of his embrace long enough to grab an order pad and a pencil.

"No, darlin', the kind of poetry I'm talking about doesn't need paper and pen," Derek said.

And he brought his mouth down on hers and showed this society girl just what kind of sonnets a soldier like him could muster.

* * * * *

Silhouette ROMANCE™

A PROTECTOR, A PROVIDER, A FRIEND AND A LOVER—HE'S EVERY WOMAN'S HERO....

He's My Hero

February 1999 MR. RIGHT NEXT DOOR
by Arlene James (SR #1352)

Morgan Holt was everything Denise Jenkins thought a hero should be—smart, sexy, intelligent—and he had swooped to her rescue by pretending to be her beloved. But if Morgan was busy saving Denise, who was going to save Morgan's heart from *her* once their romance turned real?

March 1999 SOLDIER AND THE SOCIETY GIRL
by Vivian Leiber (SR #1358)

Refined protocol specialist Chessy Banks Bailey had thirty days to transform rough 'n rugged, true-grit soldier Derek McKenna into a polished spokesman. Her mission seemed quite impossible...until lessons in etiquette suddenly turned into lessons in love....

April 1999 A COWBOY COMES A COURTING
by Christine Scott (SR #1364)

The last thing Skye Whitman intended to do was fall for a cowboy! But tempting rodeo star Tyler Bradshaw was hard to resist. Of course, her heart was telling her that it was already too late....

Enjoy these men and all of our heroes every month from

Silhouette®

Available at your favorite retail outlet.

Look us up on-line at: http://www.romance.net   SRHMH

This March Silhouette is proud to present

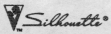 **Silhouette®**

SENSATIONAL

MAGGIE SHAYNE
BARBARA BOSWELL
SUSAN MALLERY
MARIE FERRARELLA

This is a special collection of four complete
novels for one low price, featuring a novel
from each line: Silhouette Intimate Moments,
Silhouette Desire, Silhouette Special Edition
and Silhouette Romance.

Available at your favorite retail outlet.

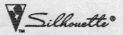 **Silhouette®**

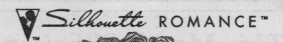

Silhouette ROMANCE™

In March, award-winning, bestselling author Diana Palmer joins Silhouette Romance in celebrating the one year anniversary of its successful promotion:

VIRGIN BRIDES

Celebrate the joys of first love with unforgettable stories by our most beloved authors....

March 1999:
CALLAGHAN'S BRIDE
Diana Palmer

Callaghan Hart exasperated temporary ranch cook Tess Brady by refusing to admit that the attraction they shared was more than just passion. Could Tess make Callaghan see she was his truelove bride before her time on the Hart ranch ran out?

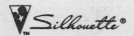

Available at your favorite retail outlet.

THESE BACHELOR DADS NEED A LITTLE TENDERNESS—AND A WHOLE LOT OF LOVING!

**January 1999—A Rugged Ranchin' Dad
by Kia Cochrane (SR# 1343)**
Tragedy had wedged Stone Tyler's family apart. Now this rugged rancher would do everything in his power to be the perfect daddy—and recapture his wife's heart—before time ran out....

**April 1999 —Prince Charming's Return
by Myrna Mackenzie (SR# 1361)**
Gray Alexander was back in town—and had just met the son he had never known he had. Now he wanted to make Cassie Pratt pay for her deception eleven years ago...even if the price was marriage!

And in **June 1999** don't miss Donna Clayton's touching story of Dylan Minster, a man who has been raising his daughter all alone....

Fall in love with our FABULOUS FATHERS!

And look for more FABULOUS FATHERS in the months to come. Only from

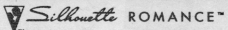

Available wherever Silhouette books are sold.

Look us up on-line at: http://www.romance.net   SRFFJ-J

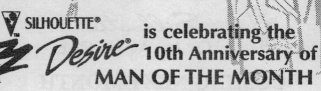
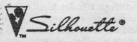

COMING NEXT MONTH